STONE COLD FOX

STONE COLD FOX TRILOGY
BOOK TWO

max monroe

Cold

A Stone Cold Fox Novel

Published by Max Monroe LLC © 2018, Max Monroe

All rights reserved.

ISBN-13: 978-1986763578

ISBN-10: 1986763579

Without limiting the rights under copyright reserved above, no part of this publication may be reproduced, stored in or introduced into a retrieval system, or transmitted, in any form, or by any means (electronic, mechanical, photocopying, recording, or otherwise) without the prior written permission of both the copyright owner and the above publisher of this book.

This is a work of fiction. Names, characters, places, brands, media, and incidents are either the product of the author's imagination or are used fictitiously. The author acknowledges the trademarked status and trademark owners of various products referenced in this work of fiction, which have been used without permission. The publication/use of these trademarks is not authorized, associated with, or sponsored by the trademark owners.

Editing by Lisa Hollett, Silently Correcting Your Grammar

Formatting by Stacey Blake, Champagne Book Design

Cover Design by Peter Alderweireld

Photo Credit: iStock Photo

DEDICATION

To the women with ambitious eyes and thirsty hearts:
You are capable of *everything*.
To the women with dry mouths and thirsty throats:
Drink water.
Or wine.
Or vodka.

To our readers:
Your hunger for Levi and Ivy's story warms our angsty little hearts.
Your hunger for tacos is what makes us friends.

COLD

BOOK TWO

I wanted a second chance. What I got was a repeat.

She was too beautiful. Too smart. And her emerald green eyes saw too much.

I wanted space—she took it away.
I craved her lips—she gave me her kiss.
I screwed it up—she got smart.

Avoiding me is the right thing to do. I'm messed up, tortured, and probably always will be.
But I still want her.
Her mind. Her body. Her heart.
I want it all.

And this time, I'm in control.
No matter what I have to do, I will make her mine.

INTRO

THE WASHINGTON TIMES

Tragedy strikes in Cold, Montana...again.
A police officer dies in the line of duty while
stopping the man the world has come to know as
the Cold-Hearted Killer.

Just twenty-four hours ago, heartbreak ravaged the small town of Cold, Montana for a fifth and final time. Detective Grace Murphy with the Cold Police Department was killed in the process of apprehending the man responsible for kidnapping and murdering four other Montana women.

October 30th, 2010

COLD—Authorities say just one month after Bethany Johnson went missing—*the fourth Cold, Montana woman within the span of seven months*—the Cold-Hearted Killer has been stopped by the heroic efforts of Detective Grace Murphy. She was too late to save twenty-four-year-old Bethany Johnson, but it is clear to everyone her sacrifice stopped this predatory serial killer from taking more lives.

The Cold-Hearted Killer has been identified.

In a press conference this morning at Cold's town hall, Chief Red Pulse officially released the name of the Cold-Hearted Killer.

Walter Donald Gaskins was a seasoned family physician for more than thirty years and the city's recently elected Coroner.

Walter Donald Gaskins was a well-respected member of the small community inside Cold, Montana and the last person these rattled townspeople expected to go on a killing spree that resulted in the deaths of five women.

"Our trust as a community has been compromised," Chief Pulse said during the early morning press conference. "No one in this town would have expected one of our own, someone we deeply trusted and respected, to be capable of such horrific acts. I can say with complete certainty it will take our small community time to heal and find closure from such a devastating sequence of events."

When reporters asked Chief Pulse about the police officer who died in the line of duty, the emotion on his face was visible to all.

"Grace Murphy was like a daughter to me. She was loved by this town. And her loss has affected us beyond words, not only because she was a fellow officer, but because she was one of us. She was family," he said before pausing briefly to compose himself. "I'm sure once the shock has worn off, grief will set in, and I pray that we as a community will come together and support one another through this very difficult time."

Questions have arisen as to why the FBI was not involved in this case, and if the Cold Police Department and Chief Pulse handled the case correctly. A spokesperson for the department maintains that since the murders did not cross state lines, it was not a legal obligation to involve national authorities.

Officials stated Grace Murphy went to Walter Gaskins's house because of a possible disturbance call on October 29th. When she'd entered the premises, she quickly found the last victim, Bethany Johnson, but unfortunately, it was too late. The victim had most likely been dead for several hours. It was after that crucial discovery, a shootout between her and Gaskins occurred.

Detective Murphy took her last breath before paramedics arrived.

Officer Levi Fox arrived on the scene for backup seven minutes later, but Grace Murphy had already received two fatal gunshot wounds to the chest. Shortly after, Gaskins received his fate by a fatal shot to the head by Officer Levi Fox.

While the names of the those involved have been released, many details still have not been.

"I understand there are a lot of questions regarding the details of this case, but I am asking for patience as we not only investigate the crime scene, but also mourn the loss of one of our own," Chief Pulse stated at the end of the press conference. "Thank you for your understanding and your time."

Many people around the nation offered condolences and prayers for the community of Cold, Montana through emails and social media posts, as well as donations for the victims' families through an online portal.

Not only is this tragedy heartbreaking, it is also disturbing.

With all of the horrific details surrounding the case, it's hard to imagine this community can rest easy tonight just because a serial killer is off their streets. It's difficult to fathom anyone could find peace in the fact that the Cold-Hearted Killer's terror didn't end with his and the victims' deaths, but instead, will reign on. His signature, his words, his official photographs will forever be on the autopsy reports of his victim's bodies.

Walter Gaskins's motives for murder are still unclear to everyone who has been following this case. Which brings us to the question on everyone's mind today—*why would a well-respected, well-liked member of the Cold community turn on his own?*

It appears, to the Cold-Hearted Killer, there was a thin line between love and pain.

PROLOGUE

Ivy

"**Y**OU'RE NOT STOPPING ME!" I YELLED, STORMING OUT OF Ruby Jane's while Levi chased after me. His footsteps, quick and harsh, sounded just as angry as his yelling had.

Loving or fighting, we could never seem to escape this place without making a scene.

"Don't be stupid," he challenged, grabbing me by the upper arm and turning me to face him. "You can't just go rogue on this. It's not safe," he said, and he lowered his voice, softening it around the edges as if I were some sort of wounded animal he was trying to lure to safety. "It's not right. And you have no idea what you could be getting yourself into."

But I wasn't a fucking wounded animal. I was a woman who would do everything in her power to find justice and to make things right, no matter what cost it might have to me.

"Oh yeah?" I sneered. "I know just as well as you do. I know as well as Bethany and Carly and Victoria and Emily *all* do." Each name that fell off my tongue might as well have been a dagger straight to my heart.

The girls. The defenseless, innocent, victimized girls.

"That's a low blow," Levi breathed, his voice rougher than normal and frayed at the edges. "I'm doing my best. Doing my best to honor them and to find *her* and to protect you all at once. God, can't you see that?"

Pain and want and desperation made my blood burn. I felt restless and manic and as if, no matter what I did, nothing would ever feel settled again.

"All I see is some macho asshole thinking he knows better than me."

Levi stepped back, dropping my arms from the X he'd formed with them against his chest. Distrust and disbelief swirled between us, and I had to work hard to keep air moving between my mouth and my lungs.

"You think that?" he gritted, all of the sapphire blue in his eyes muddied with dirty brown. I'd smeared his name and his intentions, and the insult surrounded him like a cloak. "That's really what you think of me?"

My heartbeat kicked and thudded in my chest as I considered what I knew—all of the things about the Cold-Hearted Killer I'd found out. How I had to do this to protect him.

I opened my mouth to say the word, the confirmation all that was left on the to-do list of my plan. But the wind whipped, moving his hair away from the line of his face, and his agony took over.

I was ruining this. Ruining us. And I just knew, if I went through with it, we would never be the same.

The silence was answer enough, though, filling in the word when I couldn't.

Levi's face closed down, and my heart shattered.

"Don't worry about me thinking I know better, Grace. You just proved, when it comes to you, I don't know *anything*."

Straight as an arrow, I sat up in my bed, panting and grasping the sheets at my sides. I felt overwhelmed and confused, and getting my bearings was a near impossibility.

I surveyed the empty room and eased my mind slowly, knowing none of what I'd been dreaming—none of the too-clear words, the too-familiar bleating pulse of my heart—could have been real.

All the yelling, all the heartbreak—it'd been Grace's, not mine. I'd just become so well entrenched in my character I was dreaming *as* her.

That didn't explain the depth of emotion or the ruggedly clear vision of Levi's face, but I couldn't open up a door I'd long since closed. I couldn't let myself question the decision to cut Levi out of my life for the good of us both, and I couldn't bother myself with the complications of his and Grace's fictionalized problems. I *couldn't*. I had enough to worry about on my own.

A shiver ran up my spine, and I pulled the comforter closer.

Wind bumped a small tree against the bedroom window, and the TV I'd left on hummed softly in the background.

But Levi wasn't there, and neither was Grace.

It was just me—and dreams of their movie.

A nightly routine the cruelest of powers had decided to set on repeat.

With my hands clutched around the comforter like it had the power to soothe my nerves, I stared across the dark space of the room and tried to fight against the onslaught I knew was coming. For nights upon nights, I'd been plagued with the unrest of someone else's fight, and if the routine remained consistent, this was just the beginning.

I had hours left to toss and turn and several arguments left to have. Reality would once again blur with fiction, and nightmares would catch me in their snare as soon as I closed my eyes.

The distraught look in Levi's eyes and the guttural desperation in his voice *would* find me again.

I wasn't one to believe in psychics or mediums or anything that suggested there was a way to predict the future or see the reality of the past.

But *this* dream. It shook me. To my very core.

It left me bereft in a sea of unknowns and wondering...*what if there's more to this?*

CHAPTER
ONE

Levi

THE METAL FRAME OF THE SIGN HUNG OVER THE ENTRANCE, ONLY stabilized by two, ivy-covered pillars, and beckoned visitors inside.

Cold Cemetery, it read.

As a kid, I'd liked coming here. Strolling the plots and acquainting myself with all of the people who had passed. Sometimes it was someone I'd heard of, someone I'd known through my family, but other times, it was a stranger. Someone's life I knew nothing about but could surmise—all from the things their loved ones had written about them in permanent block letters.

Cemeteries weren't known for being welcoming places, but to me, this was one of the only places all people seemed good.

Loving wives and nurturing mothers, no one ever wrote about how hollow-hearted or self-centered their relatives were. And some of them were. They had to be. I had the proof in the parents I'd been given to show for it.

Lazarus Fox. In life, he'd been an egocentric prick with little to no fatherly abilities. But here, I could almost believe he was a father, a son, and a well-respected townsperson, just as his grave proclaimed.

I moved past his headstone without pausing and through the

little gate in the middle. When we were wild teenagers, Grace and I would often sneak out of school and eat lunch on one of the stone benches beneath a big oak tree. She'd loved being there almost as much as being anywhere else, and I'd pushed her mom to get her a plot as close to that tree as possible after she'd died, instead of next to her father's grave, way on the other side.

Phil Murphy had died when she was just a toddler, in a drunk driving accident.

He was the drunk.

Grace hadn't wanted anything to do with him or his memory. Grandpa Sam had been all the father figure she'd needed.

And now, what was once our secret spot, under the shade of an old oak with life-filled leaves and roots to Cold, a place only the two of us shared, had become the one and only place I could go to see her.

Irony at its finest.

My boots crunched in the ice-covered snow as I made my way to her resting place.

Today, there was no weather; no wind, no clouds—just subzero temperatures.

The path glistened like white quartz, mere ice crystals and snow on weary concrete.

Beauty and glitz over everything dead.

The small bouquet of white roses felt weighty in my black-gloved hand.

A few feet from her headstone, I paused, and my breath rose in visible puffs.

It'd been a while since I'd come here, to her resting place. Most days I couldn't stand the quiet. To be alone with my thoughts was the complete opposite of what I found desirable in my quest to be numb. The rug was always heavy when I lifted it to sweep pain and the past underneath it, but I'd never been able to consider leaving it down to trudge over. Using the bristles to wipe away the stains and blood and heartbreak that had dirtied me in the first place.

But years of sticking to the old hollow strategy had brought me here—to a place where I avoided my own emotions and hurt people in the process. To a place where I needed Grace's wisdom about a *new* woman in my life.

I hoped the proximity to the remains of my best friend and the gift of flowers would close the gap between us for a moment, even if it was so very brief, because I desperately needed her advice.

Grace Elizabeth Murphy, her headstone read.
Loving daughter, granddaughter, friend.
True to her name, Grace was in her every step, heaven in her eyes, and in every gesture: dignity and strength and love.

Unlike some of the others, the words carved into her eternal resting place were true.

"Hi, little gem," I whispered in the still, frigid air. The sensation of the nickname leaving my lips felt foreign, and my eyes widened in surprise.

It'd been *years* since I'd said those two words.

Years since I'd been a goofy nine-year-old boy, with a special interest in letters and irony. Years since I'd noticed that the pretty girl with the fire-red hair had initials that spelled the word *gem*.

I'd found it amusing, and secretly, I'd agreed.

It hadn't taken much for anyone to realize that Grace Murphy was a gem. A truly rare, special human being with a heart bigger than the state of Montana.

That nickname had stuck, and even when she was a full-fledged police officer, the woman who wore a badge just like mine, the one who'd proven she'd give her life to save someone else, she was still a gem to me.

"Right now is one of those times I wish you were here to talk to," I whispered and ran the tips of my gloves over the edge of her headstone. "It's bizarre, I know, coming to you about another woman, but I also know you'd probably know all the right things to say."

I inhaled a deep breath and looked out across the row of headstones.

"I fucked up, Grace. I fucked up, and I hurt someone I now know means a lot to me."

Kneeling down beside her final resting place, I felt the material of my pants start to grow damp and moist from the snow-covered ground. But I ignored it, desperate to be closer to her.

"You'd like her." I laughed to myself. "Especially right now, since she hates me. I know no one knows how big of an asshole I can be better than you."

I set the bouquet of white roses down, resting them gently below her headstone.

"It's been seven days since it all went to shit. My God, Grace, you would have been horrified." A small smile curled my lips as I pictured Grace finding out what I'd done with Ivy's sister. "I'm not sure where to go or what to do, for that matter, and I could really use some help here."

I could practically hear Grace's voice and the words she would've said had she been able to respond.

You really are a son of a bitch, Levi Fox, she would've said. *Her sister?*

I rolled my eyes. Yeah, it was seriously fucked-up, I knew.

But my goal had never been more than a teasing flirtation with her sister to get under Ivy's skin. The full-fledged kiss that Camilla had placed upon my lips had been the very opposite of what I'd intended.

My heart twisted and turned inside my chest as if it was trying to escape from a vise.

The onslaught of memories was nearly too painful to process.

Camilla kissing me.

The way my mind had come to a screeching halt, trying to process what in the fuck was happening.

And when I'd finally realized how very wrong it all was and ended what Camilla had attempted to start, the look on Ivy's face when I'd locked my gaze with hers…

Her expression, the sadness and shock and pain resting behind her big green eyes, had mirrored exactly what I had felt in that moment.

Devastation.

"So what am I supposed to do now?" I asked on a near whisper, my gaze focused on the engraved epitaph of Grace's headstone. "Where in the hell do I go from here?"

Work, she would have said. *Work hard to be the man she deserves. Give her the space she needs, but stop being an asshole! I know the good version of you, and no woman can resist that man. Be him. All the rest will follow.*

A soft chuckle left my lips at the absurdity of my thoughts, thinking of what Grace would say if she were still alive.

But no matter the ridiculousness of it all, the words I'd imagined were true.

Seven days since I'd had to look directly into the eyes of Ivy Stone as pain oozed from every cell inside her body until it had coated her in nothing but agony and hurt.

Seven days since I'd fucked it all up.

Seven days since she'd last spoken to me.

One week of hell.

Grace was right. I had to do my best to prove I was something other than the asshole I'd been.

In the meantime, I'd just have to get used to the heat. I'd have to deal with all of the rage and cold silence Ivy decided I deserved to feel.

CHAPTER
TWO

Ivy

"MOVE YOUR ASS, IVY!" CAM YELLED FROM HER SPOT next to the front door. She'd been camped there for the last ten minutes, and this was far from the first time she'd yelled.

"I'm coming, I'm coming," I muttered back, in no way loud enough for her to hear me, but I didn't care. Courtesy for others was normally a priority, but my priorities had recently gone to shit. Maybe I'd care more about not making my sister wait or being early to work when I actually got some sleep again.

I scooped a random change of clothes into my bag and tied my hair into a wet knot on top of my head.

Dark circles lined the lower curve of my eyes, and my bones felt weighted with sand. Last night had been the tenth in a row where my sleep felt like more work than being awake, and my body was starting to show the effects. I was lethargic and bloated, and despite not having any time for it, I couldn't fathom going to work without showering off the thick film of sweat.

I grabbed my script notes off my dresser, slung my bag over my shoulder, and charged out of my room with way more energy than I felt. It was an act born of desperation since I really didn't want Camilla to start asking questions about my current disheveled state.

"Are you ready?" I asked without looking up, opening the handles of my bag enough to shove the script inside.

"Am I ready?" she scoffed. "That's funny, princess. I've been ready for *ages.*"

I rolled my eyes at her drama, dropped my bag to the floor, and shoved my feet into the pair of boots at the door. In an ensemble of a sweater, yoga pants, and the snow boots that had finally arrived from Amazon's wilderness branch, I should have been at the height of comfort. Instead, the shoulders of my sweater pulled at the seams, and my pants cut into my abdomen. The boots felt too tight, and a cold droplet of water poked at my neck from the tip of a loose piece of hair.

I was uncomfortable, and everything felt off.

With gritted teeth and a smile, I pulled my bag back onto my shoulder and cocked a hip. "Let's go."

Camilla's eyes surveyed the wasteland of ill-fitting clothing and bruised under-eyes and narrowed her own. "What's going on with you?"

Just like with the conversation two sisters who'd been fucked over by the same guy desperately needed to have, I did my best to avoid getting into it.

"Nothing. Come on, we're going to be late."

"Horseshit," Cam murmured.

I rolled my eyes again and reached for the door handle, but I only got it open an inch before Camilla slammed it shut.

"We need to talk."

I shook my head and grimaced. "We really don't."

"We *do*," she insisted. "It's been two weeks since that night, and all I've managed out of you is an *I don't blame you, Cam.*"

I shrugged. "Well, I don't."

"Great," she breathed. "I'm so fucking relieved. I won't worry at all then about you looking like shit and not sleeping at all and about the reasons why you both looked like you'd been gutted with an especially big serrated knife even though you'd never even really talked about him."

Her sarcasm was potent, but so was the pout in Levi's eyes every time he turned them on me. And I'd had fourteen straight days of it. I was getting *really* good at ignoring things.

I reached for the handle again and forced the door open despite her hold on it. "Glad we're on the same page."

She scowled, but Camilla was a rule-follower if nothing else. I played on her weakness for punctuality. "If you don't let me walk out the door, we're really going to be late."

"Fine," she acquiesced, giving up. "But I'm driving."

My shoulders sagged at the relief associated with her offer. If she drove, maybe I'd be able to sleep. "Works for me."

■

Happily settled into the passenger seat of my rental car, I closed my eyes and tried to find peace. Away from the turmoil of Levi's and Grace's characters, away from the heartbreak I felt from the real Levi Fox.

I was painfully close to the sweet solace of sleep when I heard the car slow to a stop and the locks sound. Surely, we couldn't have made it to the set yet, right?

Against my better judgment, I opened my eyes and surveyed the surroundings. A massive tree stood ominously just two inches from my window.

Camilla, the witch, had trapped me in, fucking engaged child safety locks and all.

My neck twinged as I swung my head to my traitor sister and

glared. "What the hell?" A simple demand but one that required an answer.

Camilla, as it was, didn't think so. Instead, she dove right into an interrogation.

"What's the real story with you and Levi?"

Pressure built in the clench of my teeth as I did my best not to shatter them. "There's no story."

Camilla laughed, rich and rotten all at once, a sickening sound of hurt and disbelief. "There *is* a story. You wouldn't be this messed up if there weren't. You wouldn't be avoiding talking to me. You wouldn't be holding me in this goddamn purgatory of unrest! What do I have to do to get you to forgive me?" Her volume had risen to a shout by the end, and the percussion pounded in my eardrums as though I were hungover.

The rubber band in my head stretched and thinned, and after a harsh bout of hell trying to avoid the truth again, it snapped.

"I forgive you, okay? Does that make you happy?" I yelled back, turning in my seat to face her. I could feel the contortion in my face as it all came rushing back and bled through the surface. Levi's lips on mine. Levi's lips on hers. A sob hitched in my throat and threatened to bring my heart up right along with it.

Her eyes flared. "Not even a little."

"Fucking great," I declared. "We can both be miserable, then!"

Her eyes turned shiny, tears pooling in the corners and spilling over onto the smooth, creamy surface of her cheeks nearly instantly.

Regret tasted like sour milk.

I reached forward and swiped the little rivers from her face with the back of my hand and ignored the piercing pain in my chest. It was screaming and twisting, an attempt to ward me off from confronting my feelings I was wholly familiar with.

But I had twenty-eight years of being familiar with my twin— twenty-nine, if you counted the nine months we'd spent inside of our mother's womb together—and I'd be damned if I was going to be the reason for her upset—sadness she hadn't earned and a whole barrel of guilt she didn't deserve—any longer.

"Stop crying, you big baby," I told her softly.

Her tears mixed in with her laugh and resulted in a snort. I shook my head.

"Ah, fuck," I sighed, slamming my body back into the support of my seat and raising a booted foot up onto the fabric. My thigh pressed into my chest, and my knee made a good resting place for my chin as I stared out the windshield at the snowy Montana back road.

Camilla was silent as I gathered my thoughts. The abandoned wilderness felt peaceful and welcoming as I lost myself in my mind and traveled back through the whole tortured story.

"Levi Fox gave me a speeding ticket on my way into town," I finally started.

I glanced her way to find her eyes wide but her mouth shut. She was riveted, as anyone hearing our sordid tale of woe would be, but she was also resolute. She would have all the goddamn answers, even if she had to sit in perfect silence to get them.

A caustic laugh. "Man, that really was the perfect beginning."

I glanced her direction once more and smiled. "I hope you've got a good excuse worked out. If I'm gonna give you the whole story, we're gonna be fucking late."

She didn't hesitate to grab her phone and type furiously to whoever needed the message, and I took the time to settle in.

Work, for today, would wait.

CHAPTER
THREE

Levi

ANTSY AND AGITATED, I BOUNCED MY WEIGHT FROM ONE FOOT to the other and chewed on the skin inside my bottom lip. It was a nervous habit I'd developed as a teenager, and by now I'd all but decimated the fragile skin. But it worked for me, giving me something to focus on internally without having to outwardly admit to any kind of anxiety.

I'd been on set for an hour and a half, and Ivy and Camilla had yet to arrive. No one else seemed even the least bit concerned over their late arrival, but it gnawed at me like an ant with a left-behind French fry.

The Lord's Prayer preached forgiveness of those who trespassed against us, but I couldn't exactly blame Ivy being slow to the godly order. I'd been trampling all over her feelings since the moment she'd come to town.

Still, that had never stopped her from being on time for work.

Normally, I wouldn't fucking hesitate. I'd have had Boyce Williams up against a wall with a hand to his throat to give me answers. And if he didn't know why she was late, to do something about finding out and quick.

But I'd been trying to think first and act later, and something told me Ivy would not swoon over the sight of me holding her producer against the wall by force.

This is insanity, Levi Fox. Congratulations, the voice inside my head taunted. *You've earned it.*

I pulled out my phone and scrolled through my phone book to Dane Marx's number. If nothing else, at this point, I needed to at least assure myself of her safety.

My thumb hovered over the call button for a long second before pressing it. And then immediately moved over to hit end as a cold burst of wind and a streak of fresh sunlight drifted in from the street.

The door swept open to reveal Camilla, followed by Ivy, entering the building with faces wreathed in smiles. Ivy looked tired but otherwise unharmed. All of my fear evaporated, replaced by relief.

I shook my head, dismayed by my inability to think of anything but the worst. I'd been doing it since Grace died, a side effect of the situation, I supposed, but it needed to fucking end already.

Cautious was one thing; paranoid was another.

Ivy buzzed by quickly, Camilla chasing after her with important notes she'd somehow already managed to acquire from Boyce, so I faded into the background and watched.

They appeared to be in rhythm in a way I hadn't noticed before, finishing each other's sentences and coming up with answers before the other even asked a question. I'd heard about twins having a kind of sixth sense for one another, but I'd never personally witnessed it. There'd never actually been a set of identical twins in Cold, Montana in the time I'd been alive, and Ivy and Camilla hadn't really been in sync before today.

Something that was no doubt my fault.

Ivy moved to the makeup room, and Camilla ventured back to Ivy's bag for something. She tossed it up and Ivy caught it without even looking back, and I became even more convinced than ever.

A rift had been burning through the uncanny connection of the twins since I'd stuck myself in the middle. But today, they'd somehow found their way back.

The door to the makeup room was still open, and I surreptitiously moved myself closer. I wanted to be a part of Ivy's chaos, to get a look into everything that went into her day and went into making her who she was.

That was how I'd spent a whole hell of a lot of the last fourteen days, honestly. She wasn't big on letting me get close enough to apologize, or more likely, argue, and I was doing my best not to push it.

After everything I'd put her through, the least she deserved was space to get her head together.

"Excuse me," Boyce mumbled as he shouldered past me on his way into the room, eyes set on Ivy.

"Hugo has some notes for you," he announced as soon as he cleared the threshold. Several heads swung over at the blaring sound of his voice, and Ivy's jerked up from where she'd been studying the notes in her lap.

Her brow furrowed as Camilla stepped forward to take them from Boyce's hand. "Is he unhappy with something I've been—"

"Read the notes," Boyce interrupted to order. "Jesus. I can't spoon-feed you everything."

I'd never considered something as innocuous as the absence of sound could occur violently until now, but silence burst through the room like an explosion.

Ivy did her best to compose herself as the rest of the room pretended to ignore the tension while still keeping an ear to the action.

I watched unabashedly, my jaw hard and ticking.

At the undeniable disquiet he'd unintentionally created, Boyce stepped farther into the room and ran a thick hand down the bare skin of Ivy's arm, leaning into her ear to whisper something none of us could hear.

Her cheeks pinked slightly, and my spine shot straight.

Goddamn, I didn't like the sight of someone else's hands on her.

Strain tightening throughout my muscles, one foot moved in front of the other, poising to step inside the room, when a small hand landed roughly on my shoulder and a taunting voice played in my ear.

"I wouldn't do that if I were you," Camilla coached knowingly. I flinched, completely surprised to find her anywhere but inside the room where she'd been before.

Obviously distracted by the interaction between Ivy and Boyce, I'd lost track of her.

"Why not?"

She jerked her head behind us and stepped away, heading across the room to the craft services table, so I followed.

Camilla moved easily, preparing a cup of coffee in a way it was obvious she'd done millions of times.

I looked on avidly for lack of anything better to do and tried to come up with the words to apologize. I was sure there were better times and ways to do it, but two weeks of time had passed and I'd yet to have the opportunity. Now had to be better than never.

"Look, Camilla—"

"Cam," she corrected without looking up.

I nodded and repeated the shortened version of her name diligently. "Cam."

She flitted from the coffee to the pastries, surveying the selection with rapt attention. I reached out and touched just her elbow. "Can you look at me?"

She shook her head without looking up. "I can, but that'll probably make my aim better when I try to stab you with this butter knife." She held it up for me to see. "So you probably don't want me to."

I chuckled despite myself. "All right. Maybe don't look at me, then. I'll settle for listening."

She snapped her fingers and grabbed a chocolate croissant from the back. "Good plan."

I rolled my eyes, but one corner of my mouth curled. "I'm trying to apologize, and you're making it kind of hard," I said frankly.

With wild hair and burning forest eyes, she looked directly at me then. "It should be hard, jackhole. You fucked up big-time."

I nodded. "I know."

Her eyes narrowed slightly. "If you really know, there probably should be more groveling."

I laughed and smiled before leaning in close and beckoning her to come closer with a curl of a finger. She did so tentatively, thrown off by my seemingly good mood. "I know I was an asshole. I was scared—"

She rolled her eyes dramatically, and I laughed again. "Cliché, right? The harsh dickhead being scared?"

"Yeah," she agreed with a comical nod. "And I have to say, dickhead is an astute observation that I fully agree with."

I shrugged. "It's all true. I was scared of love, scared of your sister, and scared of what the two of them would mean together."

Her head jerked back, and her smile melted.

"You were an easy play at the party, and in hindsight, I understand just how cruel I was. But what happened between you and me beyond the party was not my motivation or intention."

"Oh great, that makes it all better."

I nodded. "I know. It was still shitty, I still deserve for the two of you to hate me, but the way I figure it, you're going to get over it."

She guffawed. "I am, am I?"

I nodded and crossed my arms over my chest. "I was an asshole. I treated you like shit and Ivy like shit, and I regret all of it. But we both know I couldn't ever have felt something for you, as great as you are, because I was already gone for your sister."

Cam's mouth opened and closed, momentarily stunned as I leaned back in for the kill. "Forgive me?" I whispered. "I'd really hate to have a problem with my sister-in-law."

Her words were stuttered and her breathing no more than pants. "Sister-in-law?"

"I've got some work to do before then," I admitted.

Her nod was stiff and her face laughable, but the icy exterior she'd given me when we first came to the table was noticeably thawed.

I inclined my head to the cup of coffee in her hand. "Now…is that how Ivy likes her coffee?"

She nodded, analysis making her eyes turn a darker shade of green as she held it out to me.

I shook my head and smiled. "No, thanks. I watched you make it. Two sugars and a little bit of milk." She laughed—just one tiny lilt of disbelief. "I'll make her a fresh cup."

"I'll be keeping an eye on you, Levi Fox."

"By all means," I acquiesced. "If you think it's necessary, I give you permission to keep watch with two."

Just before she left to walk away, she paused her steps and turned to meet my eyes. "You really care about her?"

I nodded. "Without question."

She searched my eyes for a few long moments, assessing and scrutinizing my truth.

Until she found whatever she was looking for.

"You do something again to hurt her, I will murder you."

And that was that.

Camilla walked away from the craft services table and, ironically, her words left me standing there with a giant smile on my face.

If I did something to hurt Ivy again, I'd willingly hand Camilla the weapon.

CHAPTER
FOUR

Ivy

BOYCE WAS STILL RAMBLING ON ABOUT HUGO'S NOTES IN RELATION to being a little more clipped and rigid when I was doing my police work scenes—apparently, I'd been too fluid with my movement for his taste—but my eyes were on something else.

Camilla and Levi were standing close at the craft table, and there was a light in both of their eyes. I'd tried to stop myself from counting his smiles, but he'd already curled his lips more times than he had in the entire few months I'd known him.

And Cam wasn't exactly taciturn.

Fire raged inside my chest, licking and jumping from its origin at my heart and settling into the pit of my stomach. My jaw felt sore from the unconscious tight clench, and my hands grew clammier by the minute.

With iron willpower and a professional pep talk, I did my best to keep my attention on Boyce.

"I pushed for you to get this role, so I really need you to focus on…"

Levi reached over and grabbed Cam's elbow, and my whole body tightened.

Goddammit.

I didn't *want* to be jealous.

I didn't want to think about how at ease he was with her and how agitated he got with me, comparing the two on an endless loop. I didn't want to feel like my heart was shredding as I watched them chat and smile at one another, and I didn't want to feel myself getting angry with Cam all over again.

But she'd listened to me spill my heart about everything this morning—she'd cried with me as we'd rehashed weeks' worth of torment and a whole lot of heartbreak.

She'd understood. I'd thought she *understood*.

Why the hell is she doing this to me?

A sob threatened at the base of my throat, and I'd finally had enough. I cut Boyce off and jumped up from the makeup chair in a hurry. My makeup artist looked at me with sad eyes, painfully aware of how run-down I was on an intimate level.

There wasn't much you could hide from the person assigned to cover the dark circles under your eyes.

"Excuse me," I told Boyce, steadying my voice as much as I could manage. "I have to use the restroom."

I didn't look back as I shoved past the still-droning producer and headed straight for the bathroom.

Once inside, I locked the door and walked to the sink to look myself over in the mirror. Half made-up, contouring in place without being blended, I looked like a walking freak show. A startled laugh bubbled from my lips and turned into a hiccuping cry.

Fucking hell, I desperately wanted to splash my face with water.

But we were already behind schedule thanks to my late arrival, and having to start my makeup over from the beginning would take too much time.

Spotting the paper towel dispenser two sinks down, I furiously grabbed a handful and ran it under the tap until the brown material soaked all the way through.

I pressed it gently to the heat in my chest, hoping it would calm the fire at the source and spread to my face with time.

It calmed the edges of the rage, but unfortunately, it didn't make it all the way to the root. Frustrated, I threw the wet ball of paper into the garbage and grabbed another handful, cleaning up the sloppy mess my attempt had left behind.

Steeling my nerves and looking myself in the eye, I made a promise. A promise to focus on myself for the rest of the day instead of my sister and Levi. A promise to give the best damn performance of my life.

A promise to get the hell out of Cold as soon as this movie was done.

Resolute in my newfound inner strength, I gathered myself and unlocked the door. When I swung it open, Cam was standing there waiting for me.

"You okay?" she asked, and my acting experience kicked in.

"Fine," I advised, half in answer to her, half in a reminder to myself.

"Okay, well, Brad is waiting to finish your makeup, and Mariah called about—"

Immediately, my brain went into overload.

"Can you just handle the Mariah thing, please?"

Her eyes softened, and the corners of her mouth turned down at the grit in my voice.

"Just...whatever it is...please?"

She nodded immediately, dutiful and fully aware of my ricocheting emotions. I wasn't angry with her—I knew my sister better than that—but I didn't want her in my face either. If she left me alone and dealt with Mariah, it would serve two purposes.

"Thank you."

"Sure," she murmured, lifting a hand and giving me a squeeze on my upper arm. Her touch felt steady and grounding, and I relaxed into it a little. I didn't understand the science behind it, but Cam and I had a connection that superseded most others. No matter the rift, no matter if she was part of the reason for my chaos, she always calmed my disquiet.

I settled as she moved away with her phone already up to her ear, and I headed back to the makeup chair.

Brad, bless him, didn't say anything about my abrupt departure, and instead, went right back to work on my face with tight lips as soon as I sat down. I pulled my script into my lap and intently studied the first scene we'd be working on.

Carly Best's and Victoria Carson's bodies had been found on the same day, on the same property. We'd be moving to location for the shoot just outside of the main drag through town, but the winter weather kept most of the prep work before shooting here in the old town hall building.

I had both a trailer in the parking lot—for when the hours of shooting ran longer than the span of a normal day—and a small dressing room with nothing more than a table and a bar-height chair—where I could find a few minutes of solace in between scenes.

A cup of coffee entered the space between my script and my face, and the powerful aroma was like an instant hit to my nervous system.

God, I really needed this—

"I thought you could use a cup," Levi's rough voice said softly, curling around the edges and touching notes I'd never heard him use before.

Apparently, yelling used a different page of sheet music.

My stomach turned.

Levi's eyes softened as I accepted the cup, and I held them purposefully. I forced myself to live in the pools of blue, swim there until they heated and flashed.

And then, with a flick of my wrist, I moved the cup from my lap and dumped it directly into the trash beside my chair.

Brad's eyes widened as my gaze skirted past him on the way back to Levi.

My throat constricted on the words as I forced them up, but the effect only added to the brittle break in my declaration. "No thanks."

I expected a flare of anger—Levi's usual flash in the pan—but instead, his lips curved into a small smile. "Some other time, then."

A growl rattled in my throat as he walked away, and Brad's eyebrows rose all the way to his hairline.

"Don't ask," I insisted. "It's complicated."

Brad's smile was indulgent, but his voice was taunting. "Oh, honey. It must be."

I fought the urge for a full minute before turning to look for Levi again, but when I finally looked, my need was desperate.

The room was full, but his back stood out like a beacon.

Only then did the realization hit me.

It really *was* complicated.

It wasn't a simple situation where I hated Levi and left him in the dust. I couldn't just avoid him at all costs and concentrate on other things.

It *wasn't* over.

Because for as done with Levi Fox as my head was, my body was still charging in the other direction.

But for today, at least, I could make-believe.

One day at a time, I would pretend. And then, at the end of production, I would leave.

CHAPTER
FIVE

Levi

"QUIET ON THE SET!*"*

Silence hung in the air like that suspended moment before falling glass shattered on the ground. It felt heavy and thick against my ears as I waited for the word that instigated movement and momentum.

"Okay...*Action!*"

There it is.

Before their rehearsed lines left their lips, the near-violent pounding of my heart and unsteady inhale and exhale of my lungs boomed inside my head at a hummingbird wing's pace.

I should've been used to this by now, but I'd learned pretty quickly the silence before the words was the most terrifying part for me. Like right before a bomb detonates. It was that silence that allowed for doubt and discomfort to grow suddenly until it became a physical reality inside my bones.

"Talk to me, Grace," Johnny Atkins whispered toward Ivy, his voice loud enough to reach my ears. His big hands moved into her hair, and his thumbs caressed the silky red strands with his thumbs.

They were the only ones on set, in front of the camera's lens, inside a replica of the Cold police station.

Although the sharp, stinging pain inside my chest told me it had to be take number nine-hundred-and-two, it was only take number three for this particular scene.

And it was a kissing scene. A Grace and Levi showing progression in their romantic relationship scene.

If I'd eaten something today, I might've had the urge to vomit.

"Cut!" Hugo called from his director's chair, and Johnny and Ivy stopped, looking toward their director with slight confusion in their eyes.

"Everything you guys were doing was perfect, I'm just not thrilled with the lighting," Hugo explained. "Billy, we gotta adjust," he instructed a man with jet-black hair who I'd quickly learned was the lighting director of this production. According to the perpetual scowl etched on his lips, it wasn't the easiest of jobs.

"I need it softened up a bit," Hugo continued. "There are too many harsh lines and shadows falling over Ivy as she's looking up at him. She needs to be almost ethereal in this scene. Like heaven itself dropped a damn angel from the sky just for him."

Billy nodded, and his team of three moved their asses and got to work on adjustments while everyone else watched on with patience.

With production on *Cold* in full swing, the entire cast and crew had been putting in twelve, sometimes fourteen, hour days. Unless I had a patrol shift, I was on set nearly every day, watching in the background as Ivy and Johnny played their starring roles of Grace and me and waiting for my ride out of hell. It'd been three weeks since the clusterfuck at Ivy's house, and the burn was still so hot, I was practically smoking.

But the only chance at a reconciliation was to keep myself around. The more space I gave Ivy, the more she'd be able to build a fully fortified wall.

Plus, I'd found the more I hung around, the more useful I became.

I'd spent the better part of the morning chatting with Hugo Roman between takes, ensuring the dialogue and the way they'd laid out the events of the Cold-Hearted Killer in the script felt real to me.

The man was a perfectionist to his core. Over the past three weeks, I'd had countless meetings with him where we'd scoured every detail of the script together.

But he refused to let chance or lack of focus sully his reputation.

Where most people would be okay with a simple double- or triple-check, Hugo Roman wanted ten checks, and sometimes fifteen or twenty, depending on his mood.

I waited patiently, expecting him to call me toward his director's chair with questions, but sighed a breath of relief when I realized he was very much engrossed in something on the camera monitor.

It wasn't easy, watching the movie-version scenes of the real-life experiences that had thrown my life into a downward spiral toward complete numbness, and it was even harder giving someone pointers about how to make it more realistic. As much as I liked having an actual role here rather than standing around, it was nice to have a breather from the grief.

Before Grace had died, before Walter Gaskins wreaked havoc on our small community, I'd been a different man. Sure, I still had been rough around the edges but not so damn closed off. Back in the day, I had been a man who'd actually smiled freely and found real fucking joy in life.

After Grace had died, I'd lost it all.

I'd become a shell of myself, and I'd set my priorities on being numb—to myself, to life, to everyone and every-fucking-thing around me.

I'd changed from someone who rarely drank to someone who'd savor the moments when a few glasses of whiskey could anesthetize my feelings and quell my racing thoughts.

At least, that was how I *had* been.

Ivy's red hair fanned the room as she spun to talk to Johnny about something, and my heart kicked in my chest. Now, I was actually *living*.

Thank God for her.

Of course, living meant feeling, and as a whole, my body wasn't used to it. My bones ached with exhaustion, and my mind felt weary from the emotional and mental fatigue. I would have been lucky if I'd slept twenty minutes last night. Hell, I would have been lucky if I'd slept eight hours all fucking week.

Every night for the past three weeks, it'd been the same routine.

As I tossed and turned, my brain raced with thoughts of *her*. Her smile, her scowl—every interaction we'd had since the day we'd met.

My dreams were all Ivy, all the time, and none of them left a lot of room for actual rest.

"All right," Billy announced as he walked back off set and toward Hugo. "I think we're all set. Roll some film and see what you think."

While Hugo worked with camera angles, Ivy and Johnny stayed put on set, their bodies no longer entangled, but their eyes still focused on one another.

He said something under his breath and a soft giggle spilled from her lips and hit me straight in the chest. I couldn't *not* watch her as she quietly conversed with her costar.

She was quite the talented little actress, and if I didn't know her as well I did, I might've believed she actually enjoyed Johnny's company.

But her smile was too brittle. And her laugh was too forced.

Ivy was the type of woman where you had to work for her smiles, her giggles, her bright eyes. She didn't offer them up freely. *No.* Those reactions had to be earned.

Stubborn to her core, she was strong and determined in

everything she did, even when she was screaming at me. It was one of the things that drew me to her.

As Johnny continued to talk quietly about *who the fuck cares what*, her emerald eyes roamed off set until they locked on to me.

It only lasted a second or two, but I didn't miss it.

I relished it, actually. If anything, it gave me hope that she still cared.

"Quiet on set!" Hugo called as he situated himself back in his director's chair. "Johnny and Ivy, let's take it from the top."

They both nodded, and my eyes were graced with the horrible view of them entangled together again, Johnny's hands back in Ivy's fucking hair, his gaze locked with hers.

The set made it look later than it was, the lights mimicking night. A soft glow shone in through the only window in the frame of the camera, simulating a Montana moon, and a few gently lit lamps on the station's desks provided the light for the room.

"Rolling in three…two…one… Action!"

"Talk to me, Grace," Johnny repeated his line.

Ivy looked up at him, and her petite hands slid up his arms and stopped only when they reached his shoulders. Her green gaze searched his, and she didn't say anything until she found whatever it was she was looking for.

Johnny and Ivy. Clenched in a tight embrace. They were acting out a scene where Grace and well, I, were alone in the station, their sexual attraction toward one another reaching a point where they could no longer deny it.

Basically, it was a fucking car crash before my very eyes, one I wanted to look away from but didn't. If this wasn't masochism, I didn't know what was.

"I don't know what to say," Ivy said back, her voice soft and tender.

"Say you feel this too." Johnny gazed down at her, his normally confident and cocky eyes laced with undisguised affection and a four-letter word I'd rather not say.

"I'm scared, Levi." She swallowed, and her throat bobbed with emotion as she looked away, but his fingers were under her chin, guiding her gaze back to his.

"What are you scared of?"

"Of losing you," she whispered back. "Of us starting this, and then it not working out. I can't bear to lose you."

"You will never lose me, Grace," he said, his words ringing clear and true.

I shut my eyes for a moment. Memories, so many fucking memories, threatened to play behind my eyes, but I blinked them away. This was already hard enough; I didn't need the ghost of my past filling my head too. My heart had limits, and this, watching Ivy and Johnny acting out an intimate scene together, was already taking a Herculean effort to handle.

On the inside, I felt like a caveman. Like a man watching as his lover, his whole heart, let herself be intimate with another man without any remorse about infidelity.

I had the urge to step onto that fucking set and drag Ivy straight off of it.

Which was insane and completely irrational.

She wasn't mine.

But I couldn't help it. The emotions Ivy spurred inside of me—the pain, the remorse, the *guilt*—I had to feel every day when I saw her were nearly too much to endure.

Though, I needed to endure it. Her anger and any other bad emotion she wanted to sling my way was my fair cross to bear. I'd made this mess. I'd hurt her badly, and my impulsive, thoughtless actions that'd caused her pain had consequences.

And more than that, she needed to see that I was suffering through everything she tossed my way. My words meant shit to her at this point, rightfully so, and Ivy deserved to witness my actions. No apology or excuse or explanation would fix what I'd broken or repair what I'd lost.

I had to *show* her.

And me, sitting on this set when I didn't even need to be here, was step one.

"I'm yours, Grace," Johnny said, his blue gaze shining with affection. "Can't you see that?"

She didn't say anything, but I didn't miss the fact that her green eyes, albeit fleetingly, glanced toward where I stood off set. For the briefest of moments, Ivy's gaze locked with mine, and without any hesitation, she looked back at Johnny just as he moved his lips to hers and kissed her deeply. So fucking deep it made my chest ache with the discomfort of watching it all go down.

Those perfect, rosebud lips should only be touching my lips, my mind whispered. *And God, those soft little moans and whimpers should only be swallowed up by me.*

Even though she was acting, and it wasn't real, it hurt all the same.

And deep down, I knew Ivy wanted it that way.

She wanted me to feel the same pain that'd been tossed her way when she walked in on the sight that was her sister in my lap and her lips locked with mine.

"Cut!" Hugo Roman called from his director's chair, but Johnny and Ivy didn't stop right away; their kiss lingered for about five seconds longer than it needed to.

Eventually—a goddamn eternity later—they disentangled themselves and looked toward a smirking Hugo.

"The lighting is perfection, and what chemistry you two are giving me!" he exclaimed as he stood and clapped his hands together in three successive smacks. "I'm loving everything I'm seeing!"

Johnny smiled like the egotistical bastard he was and wrapped an arm around Ivy, pulling her into his side. "I'd love to take credit, but this beautiful and talented lady right here makes it too easy."

Ivy laughed off his half-assed compliment, but her shoulders stiffened at the first inkling of his off-camera touch.

Hugo walked onto the set and chatted with both Johnny and Ivy for a few moments, and I was thankful for the reprieve from having to watch them lip-locked, with Johnny's stupid hands all over her.

I fantasized about breaking those fucking hands of his. Finger by finger, I'd twist each knuckle back until it gave way with a satisfying snap.

It was morbid. And crazy. But it didn't change the fact that I'd thought about it. On more than one occasion over the past week, to be honest.

The break ended before it really began, and Hugo was back in his director's chair calling for another round of fucking misery.

Nausea clenched my gut. *Fuck, I don't know how much more I can take today.*

"Action!" he shouted, and instantly, I had to look away.

I knew the script, and I knew that kiss would turn heated and, well, I just preferred *not* to see the rest. My heart couldn't stand seeing Johnny Atkins's lips all over Ivy's neck, her shoulders, and even the soft swells of her breasts peeking out above her bra after he unbuttoned her uniform shirt and slid it down her shoulders.

I just...couldn't watch it.

But when I turned on my heel to stare in the opposite direction of the set, the view wasn't much better.

With a mane of red hair tossed up in a ponytail and green eyes that should be illegal, there stood Ivy's reflection, her twin sister, Camilla.

Her shoulders looked stiff, and her arms were crossed over her chest. Her normally friendly gaze moved from the set, meeting mine, and her expression was everything but welcoming.

After the conversation we'd had where I'd declared my intentions, she'd softened slightly, but she was nowhere near my biggest fan.

A conversation with her today wouldn't get me any closer to where I needed to be.

What I needed was sleep. Even though production had a day off tomorrow, I still had a patrol shift in the morning.

But I'd be back, and Ivy would be seeing me again.

Even on the days they didn't need me and I was free from a patrol shift, I'd be on set.

I'd be here until the end.

CHAPTER
SIX

Ivy

A FTER ANOTHER TWELVE-HOUR DAY ON SET, RE-RUNS OF *THE Golden Girls* provided a soundtrack to my thoughts while Camilla and I sat together on the small loveseat sofa. She watched and occasionally laughed, but I couldn't process anything occurring on the flat screen.

My mind raced as I tried to analyze every-god-damn thing.

I'd thought after Camilla and I had talked in the car, I'd found some semblance of closure.

But when I'd seen her and Levi chatting beside the craft table, I hadn't been able to stop the gushing geyser of emotions I'd yet to process.

That was a fucking week ago.

Between work and my sister and my asshole producer Boyce Williams and having to see fucking Levi Fox nearly every day, it'd been a long week.

I knew, lately, I hadn't been the most enjoyable person to be around. I knew I'd been cold toward my sister. Short-tempered and quick to get bitchy and walking around in a constant state of annoyance.

But I couldn't seem to find the off switch.

"You want to watch something else?" she asked, and I shrugged.

"I don't care." The words were frigid and disconnected, and the instant they left my mouth, I felt bad.

Silence spread over us like butter on bread, but once it melted into our pores, my sister couldn't resist taking a bite and disrupting the calm.

"Don't you think we should actually talk about what's got a bug up your ass?" Camilla asked from her cozy spot on the couch. She had a pink afghan wrapped around her body like a burrito and her far-too-knowing eyes were one hundred percent locked on me.

Fucking hell. I knew it would come eventually, but it was the last thing I wanted to do. How was I supposed to talk about things I didn't even really understand myself?

Such as, *Levi fucking Fox* and his cozy talks with my goddamn sister.

"There's nothing to talk about," I insisted.

The sigh that escaped my lungs must have weighed one hundred pounds.

"Don't be like that. You and I both know you've been icing me harder than fucking Montana winter." My sister frowned and tapped her toe against my leg. "What did I do now? Is it the kiss? I honestly thought everything was fine after we talked last week in the car, but now, well, it doesn't really feel like it. Do you still not forgive me?"

God, I didn't want to think about that stupid fucking kiss.

"Cam, we're good," I deflected, unwilling to bring up the conversation she'd had with Levi without her bringing it up first. "Nothing could ever affect our relationship."

"Are you sure about that?" She quirked a brow as if to say, *I call bullshit*, and I understood the reason. No doubt, I *had* been cold to her for the past week, despite truly believing her innocence. I knew she wouldn't hurt me any more than I would hurt her. I just needed the ache in my heart to get the memo.

"Yes." I nodded, more than certain my words were truth. No matter what was between us, we'd always be linked in a way that couldn't be broken. "You're my sister. My best friend. Nothing will ever change that, especially not some asshole guy."

She stayed quiet for a moment, only the sounds of *The Golden Girls* talking about cheesecake filling up the space between us.

But her silence was brief, and I grimaced when she said, "I was the one who kissed him. I know he's done a lot of shit, but that night he wasn't the one to make the move. I was."

I rolled my eyes. We'd already talked about all of this. She'd already explained the whole damn situation to me. "I know that, Cam."

"I know you know. But it felt like you might need reminding."

My attitude smarted at her obvious defense of the bastard. "I'll bet."

"What's that supposed to mean?"

"Nothing."

She reached over and punched me right above the boob. "No, not nothing. What the fuck does that mean?"

I rubbed at the sore spot and seethed, finally getting to the point where I was done with this shit. Done with hiding what I knew and done with her holier-than-thou approach.

"God, I saw you with him, Cam! Last week at the fucking craft table!" I yelled. "I don't know what he said to you, but you're obviously on his side."

Her eyes widened at the news but pretty quickly narrowed in offense. "What? No, I'm not! First of all, that conversation was him trying to apologize to me and own up to the fact that he was a giant fucking bag of shit to both of us. And secondly, I would *never* take his side over yours."

"You seem really fucking pushy, then," I argued.

"For *you*," she emphasized. "Pushy for you to remember all

the facts and not discount the possibility of something just because you're stubborn. Pushy for you to really think everything through instead of basing all of your anger on one stupid fucking kiss!"

"It's more than the kiss!"

Her voice was calm in a way I didn't think I'd ever be again. "He did a lot of shit to you, Ivy. But you weren't done with him. You weren't over him. Until. That. *Kiss.*"

We'd only been at this conversation for all of five minutes, and already, exhaustion seeped into my pores and made my brain feel muddled and foggy.

Maybe I should've been more willing, maybe I shouldn't have been so hell-bent on avoiding it all, but the wounds were still too fresh and oozing with the blood of my pain.

I knew it'd been nearly a month since I'd walked in on Camilla kissing Levi, but I just wasn't ready to get into it again.

I felt confident Camilla and I had cleared the air the day it'd all gone down. I'd made sure she knew I wasn't upset with her. Because, frankly, I'd had no right to be upset with her. I'd withheld any and all information about Levi, and he'd been a bastard and basically flirted her into kissing him.

And when it came to Levi Fox, I didn't give a fuck about what he felt.

"I told you before…I'm done talking about this! Levi Fox is a fucking fuck who can go fuck himself!"

She wouldn't give it up. "I know he was an asshole for making me think he was interested in me. I mean, seriously, I wouldn't mind chopping his fucking balls off for the way he used me in his fucked-up little game, but I'm not so sure you should be solely mad at him for what happened. I kissed him, Ivy. I made the move. Not him."

A softy to her core, my sister had a propensity for guilt that was frustrating. "Wake the fuck up and realize it wasn't your fault. It wasn't my fault, it wasn't your fault, and I don't give one flipping iota about Levi Fox. It's not gonna happen, so just drop it!"

I was breathing heavily and my point was effectively made, but Camilla was quiet. Her sensitivity was raw and real, and she always felt for everyone. Even the people she so very clearly shouldn't.

I gently clasped her hand tighter until her green eyes lifted to mine. I smiled and nodded. "It's in the past. You and me, we're good, and that's all that matters."

"It sure doesn't feel like it's in the past," she said and let go of my hand as she readjusted herself on the couch until she was more sitting up than lying down. "He's been showing up on set every single day, even when he's not needed."

God, I needed a reprieve from this. A break from this conversation, from my sister's guilt, from anything and everything related to Levi Fox. I feared if I kept thinking about all of it, my brain would spontaneous combust from the mere emotional overload it delivered.

"I think you need to understand that that conversation between Levi and me revolved around *you*," she added, and her voice softened around the edges.

I appreciated her honesty, I really did, but I'd reached my breaking point when it came to conversations about Levi Fox.

"You know what I think?" I questioned with a raise of my brow, and Camilla squinted her eyes at my words.

"What do you think?"

I think I need a distraction.

"I think we need to get the fuck out of this house and have a fun night out," I said and forced a soft smile to my otherwise sad lips. "We've got the day off tomorrow. Let's take a load off, have some drinks, and enjoy ourselves."

She stared at me, and I had to swallow against the discomfort from the concern in her eyes. "You really want to go out?" she asked and glanced at the clock on the cable box sitting on top of the television. "It's ten thirty. We've been up since five this morning."

"So?"

"So, I think it's safe to say I'll be asleep before we even get in the car."

When it came to nocturnal clocks, my sister and I were in completely different time zones. Her eyes always grew heavy with slumber by ten, whereas my body could easily catch a second wind.

She'd always be the morning bird who'd catch the worm, while I'd still be in bed, hoping to God she managed to snag an extra snack for me.

"You don't want to go out?" I asked, and she shook her head, pointing an accusatory index finger in my direction.

"No," she added with an amused smile. "And no amount of puppy-dog eyes or pouty lips will get me to change my mind."

Fuck, I really thought that would've worked.

"Aw, c'mon, Cam," I exclaimed on a groan. "Just one drink."

She shook her head, determined. "Nope. I'm keeping my ass right here while Sophia slings sarcastic insults toward Blanche Deveraux."

I knew if I stayed on the couch, inside this house, my sister would keep trying to talk about all of the things I very much couldn't handle talking about.

I was still processing. Still trying to figure out why in the fuck, after everything that had gone down, after the way he'd been so thoughtless and cruel, I still couldn't get Levi Fox off my mind.

I just wanted him gone. Out of my head and out of my life.

Out of my fucking traitorous heart.

All of a sudden, the walls of the house felt smaller, and each inhale through my lungs was tight and difficult.

Yeah, I needed to get out of this house before all of the emotions I was trying to keep tightly contained slipped out of their box and crashed down on me all at once.

"Okay, well," I said as I stood, tossing the remote onto the coffee table. "I'm going to head down to Ruby Jane's for a bit."

"Seriously?" Camilla's eyes widened, and I nodded. "Are you sure that's a good idea, Ivy?"

Pretty sure it was the only good idea I'd had since I'd driven into this fucking icy tundra.

"Yep," I answered and padded across the hardwood floor toward the hallway. "I promise I'll be fine," I called over my shoulder. "I'll just have a drink, chat up the bartender for a bit, and come home."

"Only one drink?" Camilla's voice filled my ears once I reached the bedroom.

"Yes. Only one drink, Mom. Promise."

Famous last words? Probably.

But did I care? Definitely not. I just needed to get out of the house before all the fucking walls crashed in on me.

■

"W-what time is it, Louie Louie?" I asked the bartender as I attempted to hop back onto my barstool gracefully and down another beer. My movements weren't as graceful as I'd hoped they'd be, but who the fuck cared, right?

At least my ass was on the seat, and I could enjoy more of this delicious beer.

I think it was a special kind of beer. Probably some rare alcoholic delicacy only found in Cold, Montana.

"It's a little after one," he said, and I pushed my lips out into a pout and nodded toward my now empty beer.

"Another, please?" I asked, and he shook his head.

"Can't do that, Ms. Ivy."

"What?" I questioned and rested my elbows on top of the bar. "You outta of this kind or somethin'?"

"We've got plenty of Budweiser, but I'm not serving any more to you."

I'm drinking Budweiser?

Surely, normal Budweiser didn't taste like it'd been brewed just for me by heavenly, alcohol-loving angels? Maybe it was a special edition kind of Budweiser, and that was why he was being so fucking stingy with it.

"Okay, I get it," I responded, and my lips crested up into what felt like a big old grin. "You're trying to save the special edition shit."

"Huh?"

I laughed. Lou was funny. I sure liked him a lot. "Don't worry, your secret is safe with me, and you can just give me something else. I'll drink whatever ya got, Louie Louie."

He shook his head again, but Jesus it was too fast. His head morphed into two heads, and I feared if he kept moving like that, he'd shake it straight off his body.

"I'm not giving you any more drinks tonight."

"Oh, shit, did I miss last call?"

"Nope."

"Then...?"

"I'm cutting you off, sweetheart," he said. "You've had enough for the night."

I pouted again. "But I'm not done."

"I'm afraid you are done."

Man, Louie Louie was being a bit of an asshole.

Cutting me off for the night? What in the fuck was that about?

"Your sister's in town now, right?" he asked, and I nodded, my face resting in my hands.

"You betcha."

Sigh. My sister was the best sister. I loved her more than anything in the whole world, even when she was trying to have serious conversations with me about the alpha-bastard I never wanted to

38

think or talk about again.

"How about you give me your phone and let me give her a call?"

"No, thank you. She's probs sleepin'." I waved him off, but my eyes fixated on the way my fingers looked like jelly as I did it. *Holy moly, I hope these hands of mine go back to normal in the morning.*

"Is this your phone?" he asked, and I looked away from my weird, wiggling and floating in the air fingers to find him holding up a cell phone.

I shrugged. "Who knows."

"It's got a picture of you and your sister on it. It's safe to say it's yours, sweetheart. What's your passcode?"

"Passcode?"

"The number you type in to unlock the screen."

"Nine…five…four…three…two…one…"

"That's six numbers," he said, the little mathematician. "It's only supposed to be four."

"Oh," I said and tapped my fingers across the top of the bar. It was a bit wet and sticky and made me giggle when my pinkie finger felt glued to the surface.

"Ivy?"

"Present!" I yelled, and it reminded me of being in high school. I laughed at the outrageous thought.

"What's your passcode?"

I squinted my eyes and looked at him closely as I tried to remember whatever the fuck he kept asking me about, but when the next song on the jukebox started playing, I knew I needed to dance.

Yeah. Dancing. That's exactly what I need to do.

"Let's dance, Louie Louie!" I shucked off my sweater and threw it toward him. "I fucking love this song!"

"Ivy! Wait a second," he called toward me as I shimmied my feet toward the dance floor.

"Be back later, Lou!"

I danced. And other people started to dance. And then it felt like everyone was dancing.

Boy, oh boy, I liked all these small-town folks.

They were my friends.

My new *best* friends.

Maybe I could talk one of them into snagging a beer from Louie Louie for me.

Fan-fabulous. Wait…Fabutastic? Fantabulous?

Meh. Whatever. It's a brilliant idea.

CHAPTER
SEVEN

Levi

ENVELOPED IN THE DARK, I WAS SO CLOSE TO MUCH-NEEDED SHUT-eye I could nearly touch it. The quiet caressed my skin like a cool summer breeze, soothing my tortured soul and filing down the jagged edges of my mind.

It had been one hell of a rough day.

And the silence within my house was a restorative draught after the frenetic rush of the day. It surrounded me like a fresh, pristine, white blanket of snow on a winter's day and smoothed away the roughness.

I'd been in bed for all of twenty minutes, but my eyes had fallen closed just as sleep started to take over. I drifted further and further toward slumber, but far off into the distance, the faintest ring started to fill my ears.

But I couldn't focus on it, couldn't rationalize what it was.

Vivid colors and figments of dreams swirled through my mind like a kaleidoscope as my subconscious hopped into the driver's seat, more than ready to take over for the next several hours.

But again, the ringing.

It got louder.

Louder.

Until I realized it was my phone.

Goddammit. I should've put that fucker on silent.

With a heavy sigh, I opened my eyes just enough to snag my cell off the nightstand. The screen was a fuzzy mess of green and black and white, and I couldn't make out shit. So, without the ability to actually screen the call, I answered by god-knows-which ring.

"Hello?" I said, voice gruff with fatigue, and closed my eyes again as I did.

"You sleeping, Levi?"

"Considering I'm talking to you, it's safe to say I'm not sleeping," I muttered, not even busying myself with the fact that I still had no idea who was calling. "Although, I sure was giving it my best effort about thirty seconds before you called."

"Ah, shit," he responded. "Well, sorry to wake you, but I need a phone number from ya."

"First, remind me who I'm talking to."

"It's Lou," he said, and confusion was laced within his voice. "Don't ya got my number saved in your contacts?"

I pulled the phone away and checked the time.

1:30 a.m.

Jesus Christ. I was supposed to be at the station at seven in the morning.

"Let's skip the pleasantries and get straight to it, Lou. What can I help you with?"

"You know Ivy Stone's sister, Camilla?"

My eyes popped open wide of their own accord. "Yeah...I know her. But why are you asking me if I know her?"

"Well, I was hop—" he started, but he paused, and a female voice filled the background.

"Louie, Louie! I need a-nother drank!"

"Everything all right, buddy?" I asked, and his answering sigh told me all I needed to know.

It sounded like Ruby Jane's was really reading him the riot act in the form of obnoxious and heavily drinking patrons.

"Not exactly," he added but then paused again. "Hold on for a sec, will ya?" he asked, but I honestly couldn't tell if he was talking to me or the drunk in the background. "Ivy, I already told you. You're cut off for the night."

Wait a minute...did he just say Ivy?

"Aw, Louie Louie! Stop bein' so mean to me!" Despite the slur distorting her words, I knew that voice, and like a racer out of the gates, I was up and sitting on the side of my bed before I even realized the gun had fired.

"Lou? You still there?"

"Unfortunately, yes," he responded, and a groan-like sigh filled my ears. "I was hoping you had Camilla Stone's phone number so I could tell her to come pick up Ivy. I'd take her home, but the bar won't close for another hour, and I just don't think it's a good idea if she hangs out here any longer. The girl needs to call it a night, if you know what I mean. Just don't want her doing anything she'd regret in the morning."

"I'll be there in ten minutes," I said, and my legs were already in motion, heading toward my walk-in closet to throw something on.

"Huh?" Lou questioned. "No need for you to come down here. I'm sure I can get her sister's number somehow. It's a damn shame she's got one of those passcodes on her phone. Otherwise, I would've already found it. Not to mention, she's claimin' she forgot the damn passcode..."

"Lou, just keep her there. I'll come get her."

"Well, okay, I—"

I didn't give him any more time for chitchat. I ended the call with a quick goodbye and slid on a pair of jeans as I did.

About a minute later, I was downstairs, slipping on my boots and jacket and grabbing my keys off the kitchen counter.

I wasn't wasting any fucking time.

The idea of an intoxicated Ivy at Ruby Jane's had my stomach all tied up in knots.

She wasn't much of a drinker. I knew that much about her. And I felt fucking horrible over the fact that her newfound love of alcohol had come only three weeks after I'd really fucked things up between us.

It didn't feel like a coincidence.

God, if something happened to her before I got there, I would feel responsible.

I knew she was an adult and she could handle her own shit, but it was pretty fucking hard for me not to feel like I had some sort of part in this.

The wheels of my truck spun in quick succession as I slipped the gear into reverse and backed out of the driveway. Once I reached the end of the gravel, I swung my truck out onto the main road, flipped it into drive, and headed toward the center of town.

Like a bat out of hell, I drove a good fifteen miles over the speed limit and didn't let up until I was pulling into Ruby Jane's parking lot.

Considering it was a Friday night, the bar—and parking lot—was filled to the brim.

Ivy won't be the only one needing a ride home tonight.

It wasn't hard to deduce the obnoxious state that lay behind the front door from the parking lot. The steady boom of bass from the jukebox and riotous laughter and chatter echoed from the otherwise tiny building. It made normally quiet as a mouse Cold, Montana seem like there was an actual rave being held inside the center of town.

Instantly, my mind flashed with visuals of the random, asshole men in town who'd be sitting in the wake, waiting to pounce on a too-drunk Ivy.

Nausea churned in my stomach.

Fuck.

Please don't let me walk into anything that will make me lose my shit, I prayed silently. The last thing I needed was to end up in some sort of bar brawl because some asswad townie was taking advantage of her.

Knuckles clenched around the worn handle, I swung open the door and stepped inside.

I didn't even have time to take a calming breath before my senses were assaulted by the smell of booze and sounds of drunken gibberish and loud as fuck music playing through the speakers throughout the bar.

But it wasn't the normal playlist I'd come to know from our little town of Cold.

It was something more relevant, the beat strong and modern and fast-paced, and the female singer's voice sexy and sultry as she sang about someone being on her mind.

Generally, the music selection revolved around Skynyrd, Garth Brooks, Carrie Underwood, and sometimes, when people were feeling a little frisky, some Zeppelin or AC/DC.

If there was one certainty in Cold, Montana, it was that these small-town folk always stuck to the classics. Pretty sure Chief Red would have a goddamn stroke if he'd walked into Ruby Jane's and had his ears filled with Justin Timberlake singing about bringing sexy back.

I looked toward the bar and met Lou's eyes.

Immediately, he nodded toward the jukebox at the back of the bar.

The instant we'd replaced the old, shabby style jukebox for a more modern, sleek design that actually accepted credit cards instead of coins, the bar patrons of Ruby Jane's had made good fucking use of it.

And obviously, right now was no different.

The only exception was that apparently Ivy Stone was involved in tonight's music selection.

I furrowed my brow and moved through the crowd of patrons drinking and laughing and singing along while their eyes stayed fixated in the opposite direction of the front entrance.

Once I waded through the sea of drunk and buzzed, the crowd parted slightly, and my boots almost flew out from under me when I caught sight of a mane of fiery red bouncing around as Ivy sang into a makeshift microphone—*an empty beer bottle.*

I glanced over my shoulder and noted just about everyone in the fucking bar was watching her shake her little hips and slur out whatever words it was she was singing.

Jesus Christ. This is not good.

The other women in the bar appeared to be entertained, even belting out the lyrics right along with Ivy, while way too many of the men seemed far too pleased with the view.

A part of me couldn't blame them. Ivy Stone was no doubt the most beautiful woman ever to step inside of this city's limits, but the most prominent part of me, the one whose rage was starting to boil inside his veins, was real fucking pissed.

With a quick flex of my knuckles, my fists clenched of their own accord.

Fucking perverts. If I hadn't been so focused on getting Ivy the fuck out of the bar, I would've been tempted to throttle each and every one of the assholes staring at her with carnal intentions in their eyes.

She was clad in only a thin, nude camisole, a pair of tight jeans, and knee-high boots, and I had a feeling she'd shucked her sweater at some point in the evening.

My gaze moved over her body, noting the very prominent swells of her breasts and the hardened state of her perfect nipples so easily seen through her shirt.

If it was possible, I grimaced and scowled at the same fucking time.

Jesus. I have to get her out of here like two hours ago.

To my left, I spotted Mikey Randall, a twenty-one-year-old little asshole who spent most of his days smoking pot and drinking booze when he wasn't busy cooking burgers at the diner. He smiled over his beer bottle and all but licked his fucking lips at his view of Ivy. The instant he pulled his cell phone out of his pocket, lifted it in front of his face and pointed it directly at her, I nearly lost it.

Quick as a whip, I snatched it out of his hands.

"What the fuck?" he muttered and turned on his heels until his irritated and very hazy gaze met mine.

"Consider this a warning," I said, staring him and the rest of his asshole buddies down. "If I see any of you trying to film her or take pictures of her again, you're going to have to deal with me."

They just stared at me, and with a sharp inhale and exhale through my nose, I leaned even closer to them.

"We clear?" I asked, and it was then they decided to offer a response, nodding and muttering their understanding.

I glared at them for another long moment, half tempted to throttle a few of them just to ease the rage that coursed through my veins, but I knew they weren't my priority.

Like a boomerang, my gaze swung back to Ivy.

I had to get her out of here.

But I had to find a way that didn't include me tossing her over my shoulder like a caveman.

Although, that plan was sounding more and more appealing the longer I stood in the middle of this fucking circus.

Without hesitation, I strode up to where she stood, still dancing around and singing at the top of her lungs, and I made my way to the jukebox without her even realizing I was there.

"Ohhhhhhh! Ohhhhhh!" she belted out, and if it was possible, my grimace grew deeper.

Jesus Christ. What a mess.

With my back toward Ivy and my gaze scrolling the jukebox, I noted she was currently singing along to "On My Mind" by Ellie Goulding. I'd never heard of it, but damn, as I listened to her screaming out the lyrics, they sure rang loud and clear.

But despite the relevance of the song, it was time to turn it the hell off and get Ivy out of there before she did something she'd regret in the morning.

Maybe my reasons were slightly selfish, but fuck, I hated seeing her like this. Intoxicated. Zero inhibitions. Completely unaware of the way the sleazy men in this bar were gawking. Not to mention, she was revealing a hell of a lot more than she would if she were sober.

Four quarters into the jukebox, I chose another song, a much fucking slower song, and over the crowd of people, I met Lou's eyes at the bar.

I nodded toward him, and without any hesitation, he switched off Ivy's performance choice. When the smooth and slow opening beats of Lionel Richie's "Hello" filtered through the speakers, the entire bar damn near skidded to a stop.

"Louie Louie!" Ivy shouted toward him, but he just shrugged.

"Sorry," he called back. "Felt like it was time for a change."

The rest of the crowd moaned and groaned their annoyance, and I used that time wisely to lure Ivy away from that fucking jukebox.

"Hey, there," I said, and her hazy emerald gaze lifted to mine. "How about we walk outside for a minute and get some fresh air?"

Surprise registered on her face, furrowing her brows and pushing her perfect mouth into a little O.

"Huh?" she questioned, blinking several times in confusion.

"Just come outside with me for a minute. Camilla wants you to come home."

"She said that?" she asked, and I nodded. "Oh, shit," she muttered to herself. "I told her I'd only have one drink, but I had lots of drinks. I'm such a shitty sister."

"She's not mad," I reassured, and with my hand at the small of her back, I led her toward the bar.

"She's not?"

"Nope," I answered, voice soft and cajoling. "Let's get your stuff, and I'll take you home."

"My car is here. I needs a car."

"I'll make sure someone drives it home for you tonight."

"Whatever," she muttered, and to my surprise, it didn't take much effort to get her sweater and jacket back on and her drunk little ass outside to my truck.

I should've known it was too good to be true, though.

The instant I opened the passenger door, her green eyes went from blissfully unaware to glaring. "I don't want you here," she spat. "You're a fucking asshole, and I'm done with you."

Straight to my chest, she metaphorically sucker-punched me. Even three sheets to the wind and slurring, her words still packed a shitload of power.

"Just get in the car, and I'll take you home."

"I don't want to go home. And I sure as fucking fuckity fuck don't want to go with you!" she shouted and shoved at my chest with two wobbly hands.

Her intentions of putting space between us did the exact opposite. With her unsteady legs, the tip of her boot got stuck in the gravel, and she tumbled toward me. Luckily, I caught her with ease and settled her back on her feet with a strong hand steadying her back.

The urge to give in to frustration was strong. I wanted to tell her she was way too fucking drunk. I wanted to tell her she was being reckless. I wanted to pick her cute, slurring ass up and toss her into my truck.

But I didn't. Somehow, someway, I maintained my control.

"Ivy, I need to get you home."

She closed her eyes, leaned her head back toward the sky, and sighed. "I don't like you."

"I'm well aware of that." Odd as it was, I had to bite my lip to hold back a smile. Even drunk as a skunk, she was a feisty little thing.

"I like kissing you, but I don't fucking like you," she whispered, and her eyes popped open, their hazy depths locking with mine.

I had no idea how to respond.

But it didn't matter.

With alcohol flowing like a river in her veins and zero inhibitions holding her back, Ivy moved like a rocket, hopping into my unsuspecting arms and wrapping herself around me like actual ivy. Lips to mine, she kissed me.

Hard.

Deep.

And before I could stop her, her tongue slipped into my mouth and urged a moan from my lungs.

Emotion tightened my throat, and I nearly wanted to cry.

She felt so good. Tasted so fucking good. And I couldn't stop myself from kissing her back, from sliding my hands under her curvy little ass and pulling her tight against me.

We kissed.

And then, we kept kissing.

In the deep recesses of my mind, I knew I needed to stop it.

But God, I'd missed her.

She all but clawed at my clothes as she ground those sexy hips against me. My cock grew hard and impatient at the feel of her, and I knew, *I fucking knew*, I had to stop before things went any further.

It took every ounce of strength I had to pull back, to slowly disentangle us until her boots were back on the ground.

Her green eyes were on fire when they met mine. Not with lust or want or need, but with anger. And maybe even hate.

"I get it now," she said, her voice surprisingly firm and steady. "Feeling like fucking and actually feeling something *are* two different things. I get it now, assface," she said. "And guess what? I don't feel shit for you."

They were like a knife straight to my heart, and all I could do was let her cruel words sink in and settle into my chest. But, the worst part of all, I deserved it.

With a deep inhale through my nose and an exhale from my lungs, I focused on my priority. Getting Ivy home safely.

"Let me take you home." I opened the passenger door to my truck and gestured for her to get inside.

She didn't respond, but she listened.

Thank fuck.

Albeit, she complied while simultaneously refusing any help from me as she awkwardly climbed inside, but it was a step in the right direction.

By the time I slid into the driver's seat and turned on the engine, I glanced over to find Ivy's eyes closed, her head resting against the window, and her mouth slack and parted.

Out like a fucking light.

I guessed it was better than her awake and drunkenly spewing hate toward me.

As I pulled out of Ruby Jane's and onto the main road toward Grace's house, I looked down at the clock to find it was a quarter after two.

Fucking hell. What a long fucking day.

CHAPTER
EIGHT

Ivy

THE ACHING IN MY SKULL EBBED AND FLOWED LIKE A COLD TIDE, yet the pain was a strong, unwanted constant. I felt like the blackest of clouds hung thick and heavy over my head with no intention of clearing any time soon.

Ow. Fuck.

With a groan and a turn, I shifted onto my side only to find I was on the couch in the living room. Camilla stood over me, her eyes filled with equal parts amusement and concern.

"Rough night?" she asked, and I groaned again.

"What time is it?"

"A little after two."

"In the afternoon?"

"Yep," she responded, popping her p with a satisfying press of her lips.

Holy shit. I'd slept the whole fucking day away?

"Jesus. I feel like there is a tiny man inside my skull with a drill and an ice pick."

"I'm pretty sure what you're feeling right now is what most people would call a hangover."

God, how much had I drunk last night?

I searched my brain for answers.

I remembered going to the bar.

I remembered talking to Lou.

I remembered drinking beer.

A lot of beer, actually. And liquor.

The memories grew hazy, and I couldn't remember much after I'd asked Lou for a shot of tequila.

Shit. No wonder I felt like death warmed over.

Wait…how did I get home last night?

"Tell me I didn't drive home last night," I said, but my voice was too fucking loud for my own ears, and a sharp sting of pain radiated across my entire face. I grimaced and groaned some more as I angled up to a sitting position.

The room moved and spun, and nausea clenched my gut from the sudden motion. With my elbows resting on my knees, which were still clad in last night's clothes, I shut my eyes and put my head in my hands.

The couch shifted beside me as Camilla sat down, and I had the irrational urge to smack her for moving around so much.

I peeked one eye open and peered at her from beneath my hands, and she offered a comforting smile.

"You didn't drive home last night."

Thank God.

But before I could ask her any more questions, my stomach rolled and swirled with nausea, and I knew that the illustrious time anyone with a hangover dreads was about to occur.

"Oh God," I muttered, lifting my head off my knees and slapping a hand over my mouth.

"You okay?" Camilla asked, but there was no time to respond.

Quick and unsteady, I hopped to my feet, damn near tripping over the afghan in my lap as I did. As fast as my legs could take me, I made a mad dash for the bathroom. Vomit slid up my throat, and I barely made it to the toilet in time for the painful purge of anything and everything I'd poured into my body last night.

Heave after heave, I prayed to the porcelain gods, my body shaking from the assault.

Good Lord, why did I drink so much last night?

It felt like hours, even though it was probably only a few minutes.

Eventually, my stomach settled enough for me to lift my head away from the toilet and swipe a shaky hand across my face, brushing away the rogue tears running down my cheeks. Drained, sweaty, and too weak to stand, I sat on the cool tile of the bathroom floor and mentally berated myself for overdoing it so much.

This hangover felt like a goddamn balloon beneath my skull, slowly being inflated until the pressure mounted to a near intolerable ache.

Never again, I told myself the same lie everyone told themselves after a drunken night. *I will never drink that much again.*

My joints creaked and popped like an old wooden chair as I pushed to my feet.

I swished the bile out of my mouth and splashed cold water onto the clammy skin of my face just to feel something refreshing, and instantly, I wished I could wash my brain free of the toxins too.

One glance in the mirror and the woman staring back at me was a sad, pathetic shell of herself. Her normally bright eyes were a lattice of pink and bloodshot, and the normally smooth skin of her cheeks appeared ruddy and devoid of life.

I cleared my throat, and it felt like sandpaper scraping together.

Basically, everything hurt.

It hurt to move. It hurt to swallow. It hurt to blink.

It was like the flu, only self-inflicted. Which meant I deserved no sympathy from anyone. Not even myself.

"You okay?" Camilla called from the living room just as I found the strength to step out of the bathroom.

"I've been better," I muttered and shuffled my feet across the hardwood floor until I could plop my pitiful self back onto the couch.

Just as I sat down, my ass vibrated, and I startled at the feel before realizing it was my phone. I moaned my discomfort as I lazily tilted to the side and pulled it from my pocket.

With one glance at the screen, I found a text notification from an unknown number. A lazy tap of my index finger and I pulled up my inbox and had to blink almost three times just to focus my eyes to read the message.

Two messages, in fact.

Unknown: Just wanted to make sure you're doing okay today.

Unknown: This is Levi, by the way.

Shock consumed me. Of all the people I expected or *wanted* to see a text from, this man was at the very bottom of my fucking list.

How had he gotten my phone number?

Confused, I looked toward Camilla and held the screen of my phone so she could read it.

"Did you give Levi my phone number?" I asked. "And why is he asking me if I'm okay?"

"No, I didn't, but..." She paused for a moment as her eyes searched mine. Eventually, she lifted her brows in surprise. "You really don't remember?"

"Don't remember what?"

"Levi is the one who picked you up from the bar last night and drove you home."

Hold the fucking phone.

"What?" I questioned, even though I understood every word

that'd left her lips.

"He brought you home last night, Ivy," she said, her voice a little too soft for my liking.

"Was he at Ruby Jane's too?"

"No." She shook her head, and her red locks slid across her shoulders. "Well, he wasn't there drinking with you. He only went down there to pick you up and make sure you got home safely."

I narrowed my eyes. "How in the hell did he know I was there?"

"The bartender called him."

God, how drunk had I gotten last night?

I searched and searched the recesses of my brain, but it all felt like a muddled mess locked tight inside a black hole.

"It was actually pretty sweet, Ivy," Camilla added, but before she could say anything else I most likely did not want to hear, three knocks to the door gave her pause.

She rose to her feet, and with a turn of her wrist, she opened the front door. A vision of red and white roses filled the view, until a man dressed in an FTD uniform lowered the floral arrangement to his waist, revealing his face and chest.

"Uh…can I help you with something?" Camilla asked, and he offered a full-toothed, friendly smile.

"I have a delivery for an Ivy Stone."

Too surprised to question, I stood and walked over to the door, stopping once I was shoulder-to-shoulder with my sister.

"Mind signing here for me?" he asked, and simply at a loss for words, I nodded and grabbed the stylus from his hands.

Sloppy and quick, I signed my name, and before I knew it, the front door was closed, and Camilla and I were staring at one huge fucking bouquet of roses sitting on the dining room table.

She snagged a small white card tucked inside the bouquet and read it aloud.

"Ivy, your beauty takes my breath away. I crave to look into your eyes. I crave to kiss your perfect lips. Love, Me."

"Me?" I furrowed my brow. "Who the fuck is me? And more than that, not many people know that I'm in Cold, Montana right now."

Crave to look into my eyes?

It sure as fuck didn't ring any bells.

Crave to kiss my perfect lips?

Until it did.

Kiss. That four-letter word spurred an onslaught of memories to flood my brain like a goddamn hurricane.

I'd kissed Levi last night.

I'd thrown myself into his arms, and I'd kissed him until he wouldn't let me kiss him anymore.

Oh, *fuck.*

I organized the details inside my head.

I'd kissed him last night.

He'd driven me home from the bar.

He'd somehow gotten my phone number and texted me this morning.

Like cold water was being tossed at my face, I startled from the surprise of it all.

Had he sent me fucking flowers too?

CHAPTER
NINE

Levi

THE WHEELS OF MY TRUCK SLOWED TO A STOP AS I PULLED INTO the driveway of my not so humble abode. Instantly, I pulled my phone out of the cupholder and checked it once again for messages.

Well, a message from one person in particular.

Ivy.

Her number had been in my phone for what felt like ages, but not because she'd willingly handed it over to me.

To be honest, I'd illegally obtained it when I'd written her a speeding ticket that fateful day she'd driven into town with a heavy lead foot and those mesmerizing emerald eyes that could bring any man to his knees. *Especially* me.

Don't ask me why I'd thought it was a good idea to program that number into my phone. But I'd done it. And that day, for reasons I hadn't understood, it had just felt like something I had to do.

God, last night had been one for the history books. Between her sassy fucking mouth and the way she'd kissed my lips and pressed herself against me, I still didn't know which way was up or down.

But I knew, despite her harsh words and all of the anger she glared my way, she still felt *something*.

Who would've thought her drunken outburst and irrational behavior had only given me hope?

Talk about a fucking paradox.

I'd texted her early this morning, before I'd started my patrol shift, just to see how she was feeling, but I'd yet to receive a response.

With one tap to the green icon, I scrolled through my messages to find a text from Jeremy asking me to babysit the girls next weekend, and I made a mental reminder to call him later.

I scrolled some more, even though I knew it was a completely lost cause.

But I couldn't stop myself. No matter how absurd the behavior.

It was like, subconsciously, I thought by checking for a text from her every fifteen minutes, I'd somehow will one to be there. Obviously, that wasn't how things worked.

Empty-handed and not a single peep from Ivy, I hated how melancholy that realization made me feel.

Fuck, this is exactly why I enjoyed being numb all the time, I mused, but I quickly pushed that toxic thought out of my head.

Even feeling like *this*, being inside this dark space of unknowns and anxiety and mental anguish of not yet fixing things with Ivy, was still better than feeling nothing at all.

With squinting eyes, I peered through the windshield and took in the clean and rustic lines of the far-too-large residence.

Every time I took a moment to actually look at my house, I thought the same thing.

Too fucking big.

Five bedrooms and three bathrooms on five acres of Montana land, it was too much space for one person.

After my father died, I should've sold it off, but something inside me just couldn't let go. I knew with every ounce of my being this house had been built with my mother in mind. Every aspect of the design itself had her taste and style and, basically, everything she had dreamed of when she had still been a part of our lives.

Lazarus Fox had built this home several years after my mother had left us to find greener and more successful pastures in Hollywood. She'd left when I was young and my father barely had two dimes to rub together.

She'd left when we'd needed her the most.

When I'd needed her the most.

Once she'd become a mere ghost of our past, my father had changed, and his priorities shifted from a man who just wanted to provide for his family to a man who wanted to obtain as much money as humanly possible. And he'd more than achieved that goal by the time he'd taken his last, dying breath.

But at what cost?

Our relationship, father and son, had been rife with turmoil and misunderstanding and a constant back-and-forth of rage and anger. And now, looking back on things through an adult's eyes, I realized my rebellious streak had just been a kid trying to get his dad's attention.

Bitter to the core, the reminiscence of my past always left an awful aftertaste in my mouth.

With a quick shake of my head and a hard swallow, I pushed the painful reminders out of my mind and shut off the engine with a quick turn of my wrist. Although this house didn't feel much like a home to me, it was still my house, my only place of refuge from the outside world.

Eight and half hours in the trenches of police work and I was more than ready to withdraw from the hustle and bustle of everyday life and savor some peace and quiet.

My boots to the ground, I slipped out of the driver's seat and shut the door behind me. As I walked toward the house, I paused to take in the pristine landscape that was my home state of Montana.

The house faced away from the center of the city, and for as far as the eye could see, green pastures, rolling skies, and lush mountains created a breathtaking view. A little slice of serenity wrapped up in a big, beautiful nature bow.

Once I stepped into the foyer, I quickly decided I needed to bask in that delicious fresh air. It'd been a while since I'd chopped some logs for the fireplace, and since the temperatures were still bottoming out in the low teens at night, firewood replenishment was a grand idea.

Plus, my head felt all fucking muddled. I needed a distraction.

Ten minutes later and I was out of my police uniform and standing outside in a pair of boots, jeans, and a thermal flannel shirt.

Ax in hand and fresh wood set up and ready near my feet, I got to work.

Forward momentum coming straight from my core, I swung the ax until the first satisfying slice and chop of wood reverberated through the cool air.

Internally, I smiled.

Hell, I might've been smiling externally too.

But my focus was otherwise occupied on the simple task of firewood, and I loved every minute of the escape it provided.

Chop after chop, I worked until my muscles were hot and burning with fatigue and sweat dripped down my brow. My breath fogged out in front of me with each heavy exhale, and I kept at it until my body screamed its need for a break in the form of shaking hands and weak legs.

Placing the sharp point of the ax to the ground, I leaned against the house and guzzled from the bottle of water I'd set on the windowsill when I'd first come outside.

Eyes to the sky, I took in the view. Overcast and cloudy, it looked like a child had started to draw on it with a pencil, but then erased it away into smudged gray.

Just as I set my water bottle back on the windowsill and grabbed my ax for round two, the sounds of wheels crunching across gravel caught my attention.

The crunching grew closer until it stopped.

Who in the hell is here?

I furrowed my brow in confusion as I walked toward the side of the house and stopped dead in my tracks once I reached the driveway.

Ivy.

Fast as a whip, she hopped out of her rental car and slammed the door shut behind her with a hard smack and a clang.

When her green gaze met mine, she glared so hard I thought, any second, she might light the yard on fire with the sheer force of it.

"Levi Fox!" she yelled toward me and shook what looked like a big bouquet of flowers in her hands. "We need to talk! Right fucking now!"

Madder than a hornet, she strode toward me, and I'd be a liar if I said I didn't feel a sudden rush of pleasure spill into my veins. My heart pounded inside my chest as she stalked toward me, her boots pounding the ground with each determined step.

Fuck, she was pissed.

And hell if I didn't love it.

I'd only get worried if Ivy turned apathetic toward me.

But, anger? Yeah. I'd take her anger any fucking day of the week.

CHAPTER
TEN

Ivy

ONE MINUTE, I'D BEEN AT THE HOUSE, TALKING TO CAMILLA about what Levi had said to her—not only last night when he'd dropped my drunk ass off, but also on set when I'd seen them chatting near the craft table—and the next I'd been calling production to get his home address under the pretense of having to ask him some movie-related questions.

Apparently, he'd been making it a point to be sweet as pie to my sister.

But not in the flirtatious, charming way he'd been at Grace's birthday party when his intentions had been toxic and thoughtless. *No.* He'd been a gentleman by way of apology and open acceptance of the way his actions had affected her.

And my sister had swallowed up his words like they were verses from the Bible.

When she'd started using words like sincere and nice and kind and sweet in relation to Levi, the first inklings of irritation had started to creep into my pores and infect my otherwise relaxed mood.

Sure, I'd been hungover as fuck, but after I'd managed some eggs and coffee, I was starting to perk up.

Things were looking good.

Until Camilla wouldn't stop talking about Levi.

Sensitive to her core and with a heart as big as the Pacific Ocean, my sister was a fucking softy, and oftentimes, felt everyone deserved a second chance.

I, on the other hand, could hold grudges like it was my day job.

And when it came to apologies, words generally meant shit to me.

I was an "I have to see it to believe it" kind of girl.

By the time my sister started suggesting I talk to Levi about what had happened, I was annoyed beyond comprehension and couldn't stop staring at those stupid fucking roses that'd been delivered to me a few hours earlier.

It was a blur after that.

I'd gotten his address. Thrown on some clothes. And gotten in the car.

Camilla thought I was going in a civil state of mind.

But in reality, I was fuming, and civility wasn't on my agenda in the slightest.

And now, there he stood, looking as handsome as ever in jeans and a flannel that showed just enough muscle for every woman in America to do a double take. Like some sexy alpha-lumberjack lifted out of the pages of a romance novel.

The fucking bastard.

I hated how good he looked.

With the stupid flowers in my hands, I strode toward him with a laser-sharp glare pointed directly at him.

I wanted him to look scared as I stalked toward him, but if anything, he just looked smug.

That only made me angrier.

The instant I reached him, I gripped the vase in my hands, and with a hard slosh, I tossed the water and roses directly at his face. With a splash, the water soaked his skin and flannel shirt, while the roses fell around us unceremoniously like limp noodles.

"Wow," he muttered, and the slightest hint of a smirk lifted the corner of his mouth. "You brought me flowers?"

If it was possible, my glare grew harsher, harder, until I could literally feel a vein in my forehead popping out to say hello.

"No," I spat. "I'm merely giving you your fucking flowers back. I don't want them."

"What?" He wiped droplets of water off his face with the sleeve of his shirt. "Giving me my flowers back?"

"Don't play coy, Levi," I said, and his brow furrowed. "And, for the love of God, don't send me flowers again. Don't text me again. In fact, don't do anything related to me. Just leave me the fuck alone."

"I didn't send you flowers."

Wait...what?

"What?" Now it was my turn to be confused.

"Those flowers," he said and pointed to the flowers on the ground with a long, straight finger. "They were not from me."

"You didn't send these?"

"That would be a negative," he said, and I hated how fucking amused he was by the whole thing. "Did they happen to come with a card?"

"Yes."

"And did you happen to read it?"

"Don't be a sarcastic dick." I shoved one harsh index finger into his chest. "And yes, I did look at it. They were signed by *me*."

He scrunched his nose. "You signed the card for the flowers that were delivered to you?"

"Oh. My. God." I wanted to scream and groan at the same time. "The card literally said '*Love, Me*,'" I explained and air quoted the mysterious signature with my fingers.

His eyebrows drew together, and his lips pressed into a firm line. "Who the fuck is *me* supposed to be?"

"I thought it was you."

He shook his head. "Definitely was not me."

So...what is he trying to say? He would never send me flowers?

Irrationally, I hated how quickly he pushed off the thought like it was an abhorrent thing to send me flowers.

And then, rationally, I hated myself for even thinking about Levi thinking about sending me flowers.

Talk about a mindfuck.

"So, I guess this means you're feeling better after last night?" he asked and then followed it up with, "You're welcome for making sure you got home safely, by the way."

Apparently, he took my lack of verbal response as an opening to rile me up.

Which, it did.

I didn't need to thank him for shit.

I didn't ask him to come down to the bar and get me. If I'd have been sober, he sure as shit would've been the very last person I would've called for a ride home. Hell, I would rather hitch a ride from a goddamn cow than get inside Levi's truck.

"Pretty sure I didn't ask you to pick me up," I said through gritted teeth. "You chose that on your own."

"Well, considering you were three sheets to the wind and one beer away from possibly getting your tits out for the skeezy men of Cold, I'd say my presence and rescue were much needed."

"Fuck you!" I shouted before I could even process the words that were coming out of my mouth.

"Oh, don't worry, you made that pretty clear last night too," he said, and I wanted to smack the smile right off of his cocky fucking face. "Pretty sure your exact words were something along the lines of wanting to fuck me but not feeling something for me."

"Boy, those words sure sound familiar," I said, and sarcasm oozed from my voice.

He laughed at that.

And instantly, I saw red. Like, crimson and fire and hell and fury kind of red.

Before I could stop myself, I dropped the vase to the grass, and with one hard, determined hand, I slapped him clear across the face.

He didn't react and I had the urge to do it again, but his strong fingers wrapped around my wrists before I could even lift my hand.

When I attempted again with my free hand, he did the same thing until he had both of my hands pinned behind my back.

"Pretty sure I've received enough of those from you to last a lifetime, sweetheart."

"Fuck you!" I screamed again. All of the pent-up anger had reached its breaking point, boiling and bubbling to the very tippy top. The fire and fury spilled out in the form of harsh words directed straight at him. "I hate you! I hate you! I fucking hate you, Levi Fox!"

"No, you don't," he retorted, and his voice dropped to a near whisper. "You're mad at me. And you have every right to be. But you don't hate me."

I jerked my hands away from his hold and stepped back to put some much-needed distance between us. But instead of space, I put on a clumsy display. My goddamn boot caught on that stupid fucking vase, and before I knew it, I was practically in the air, and my ass was headed for a crash landing on the grass.

Quick as lightning, Levi was there, pulling me into his arms before I hit the ground.

Eyes wide and lungs panting, I stared up at him.

And those fucking midnight-blue eyes of his looked down at me. I hated those eyes. Hated them so much that I couldn't seem to stop looking into them.

They were so painfully beautiful, they urged a hitch in my breath and a quickened thump-thump-thump of my heart.

And then, without thinking, and defying all rational thought, I just…kissed him.

A-fucking-gain.

I moaned and he moaned, and before I knew it, our kiss turned deep and hard and unrelenting. Our mouths were hot and greedy, and our lips and tongues danced that oh so familiar rhythm we always seemed to fall into.

I savored the feel of his soft, full lips and the way they expertly worked against mine. I savored the way his strong arms held me against his chest and the way I felt so safe inside his embrace.

He felt so good. Tasted so good. And I just savored our kiss. Too long. Not long enough. I had no idea how much time had passed.

But, eventually, the remnants of our reality started to creep into my brain, and once cognizance found its way inside, I wrenched myself away from him.

I scrubbed a hand down my face, once, twice, three times, before I finally found the strength to look up to meet his midnight-blue gaze.

God, what the fuck was wrong with me? Why was I so fucking drawn to him that my brain turned stupid whenever I got too close?

I needed help. And possibly therapy.

"This can't keep happening, Levi."

"I disagree," he retorted. "Shit like this doesn't just keep happening by chance."

"Well, I can tell you with certainty, that was the last fucking time."

He quirked a questioning brow, and I could literally hear him inside my head saying, *Are you so sure about that, sweetheart?*

Yes. Goddammit. I *was* sure.

That was the last fucking time.

"This, *us,* no fucking more," I all but yelled directly into his face. "I'm done. We are *done.*"

He didn't respond, just kept looking at me, so I added to it. "Do not call me. Do not text me. Just leave me alone, okay?"

"And what about at work?" he asked. "What should I do there?"

"Stay the fuck out of my way."

"And if you need something from me? Need to ask me something about Grace?"

God, he was infuriating.

I had to leave before I smacked him again.

"Just leave me the fuck alone!" I screamed. The end of my sentence was punctuated by passion and frustration, and the heavens saw fit to cry.

One drop turned into two, and two turned into a hundred. It was just above freezing outside, a goddamn heat wave for Montana, and as a result, snow turned to rain. It didn't come on slow with a gentle lull, but rather, ramped up the way Levi and I often did into conversation. From zero to full roar in an instant, the clouds let loose and coated both of us in liquid.

But the wicked need to yell in his face didn't melt as a result, and he made no move to retreat.

Instead, we stood panting and poised, ready to go another round.

CHAPTER
ELEVEN

Levi

MASCARA STREAKING HER CHEEKS ALONG WITH THE TRACKS OF the rain, Ivy stood her ground in the torrential downpour and faced me down.

She was beauty and agony and fury all in one; but she wasn't apathetic.

Just like the arguments of our past, the viciousness of her words and the passion of her yell were rooted in something. *I knew.*

Since the moment we'd met, when I'd been screaming at her, I'd been doing it to keep myself from saying and doing the things I didn't want to admit. I'd been scared of what could have been in the future, and I'd been scared to confront my past.

She didn't trust me, now more than ever, and her reasons were clear.

But the reasons for me to fight it were even clearer.

I'd spent weeks being gentle with her, trying to tiptoe around the wide circle of space I'd thought she'd needed. But gentle wasn't how we'd started. We hadn't eased into each other's hearts. *No.* We'd gotten under each other's skin, inside one another's souls because we'd fought our way there.

And that was exactly what I needed to do now.

I needed to fight. For her. For *us*.

"Go ahead," I told her. "Scream this fucking place down. There's no one out here to hear you anyway."

My house was secluded the way Grace's old property was, only more so, thanks to the wealth of my father and his desire to flaunt it. He'd wanted more property, more influence, a bigger house—anything he could wield over someone else.

Water clung to Ivy's shirt and forced it tight against her skin, the heat of her body steaming into the cold surrounding air. She was shivering and drenched, but this—this argument with me—was important enough to ignore it.

"Is that a threat, Levi?" she challenged, turning the line of my jaw harder. She was instigating, poking at my weakness by suggesting I was the kind of man who would use all of this space and privacy to take advantage, I knew, but that didn't stop it from smarting.

"I don't know," I shouted back over the roar of the sheeting rain and wind. "Sure seems like you've decided it is."

She charged, closing the remaining distance between us and shoving me in the shoulder. I rocked, but by and large, her push wasn't enough to make me move.

"Don't you dare," she gritted, pointing an angry finger right in my face, "turn this back on me."

I grabbed her finger quickly, forcing it down and hooking an arm around her hips.

She was too easy to move, her weight far lighter than that fucker of a producer pretended it was, as I tossed her over my shoulder and clamped an arm across her legs.

"Hey! Put me down!"

I ignored the yells easily, so she kicked and fought instead. Tenderness pooled under the violence of her fists on my back, and the toes of her boots connected more than once with my thighs, but I didn't slow.

Across the drive and through my door, I listened as she railed against every angle of my character she could manage.

Apparently, I was a bastard with no respect for women, an egomaniac with no regard for others, and a sadist with no sense to move on from these arguments between us.

She swore up and down that she was different, that she'd moved on from this twisted thing between us, and it was time for me to do the same.

When I made it to the second floor and down the hall to my room, I turned on the tap to the shower and dumped her in, fully clothed, before the water even began to warm.

Montana weather in the dead of winter was frigid at best, but add an unexpected rain shower into the mix and it might as well have been a recipe for frost bite.

Not only did Ivy need to warm up, she needed to calm the fuck down. Her panting, erratic breaths and the thrumming, hard pulse at her neck were evidence of her current chaotic state.

"Just get over it!" she yelled, raw and ragged, her voice tiring from all the yelling even if she wasn't. I turned my back on her, intent to leave her to it, but she didn't want to be left to herself. She wanted a battle, and she wanted it with me.

"Me and you aren't a thing. We're nothing. You're *nothing*."

The insulting word froze me for a fraction of a second, and then…I wasn't frozen at all.

In three short steps, I crossed the ornate tile back to her, stepped under the spray and trapped her against the shower wall.

The tile was cold, and the raining water steady as I pushed my body closer to hers and put my hands to the wall at the sides of her head.

She shook in the small space—whether it was from the cold or the closeness was anyone's guess.

"Oh yeah?" I asked, my voice low and deep.

"Yeah," she spat back, testing my limits and daring me to be the one to give in to the misplaced sexual tension.

We fought as a means to fuck when the other person wasn't willing to give in. So seemingly opposite, but so obviously established in the same thing—passion.

I smiled and embraced the feelings of uncertainty and hope— *thrived* in the same mess that'd sent me running in the first place. The difference in then and now was so finite in its simplicity.

This angry, desperate version of Ivy was a mirror of me, held up for my scrutiny as I studied the reflection and learned what I looked like from the outside.

She was teaching me perspective. And in the end, when she finally understood the symmetry of our journey to one another, she would comprehend true empathy.

"I'm not the one who drove all the way to my house and practically challenged me to a duel, honey." I leaned in closer, just skimming her lips with the wet skin of my own. "I think maybe you care a little more than you let on."

"I *cared*," she contested. "I stupidly let myself care about you, about how you were coping, about getting to know you…" Her lips shook, and an angry tear escaped, mixing with the droplets from the shower and disappearing forever. "I *cared*. You didn't. So, now, neither do I."

Fierce and cutting, her distinction was effective in all the ways she wanted. It broke down the reserves I'd built for this fight and left me hollow, and all there was left to do was give her the peace I'd so desperately wanted when I was in her position.

Her chest rose and fell rapidly when I freed it of the weight of my own and cleared the spray of the shower. It'd warmed to a steamy temperature now.

"I'll leave some clothes on the bed," I murmured. The lines of her face were warped as she tried to shroud what lay beneath it from me.

She didn't want me to see the sadness. She didn't want me to see the conflict. She didn't want me to see the pain.

All of those were weapons better wielded in secret, and I owed her the luxury.

My clothes stuck to my skin as I tracked water into the closet and set about replacing them. I didn't consider or choose, rather grabbing the first shirt, underwear, and pants I came to. But when I was through and the task was undeniably changed, so did my behavior.

Carefully searching drawers and hangers, I scoured the entire closet to find the best outfit to suit Ivy's size and comfort. My oldest Cold PD T-shirt, my favorite forest green sweatshirt, boxer briefs, pants, and a pair of warm socks. I gathered the stack of it and made my way back into the bedroom to set it at the foot of the bed.

Water slapped at the glass door of the shower, and I closed my eyes against the urge to look back. The bathroom door was wide open, an oversight on my part, and her wet clothes, violently discarded, no doubt, straggled their litter all the way into the bedroom.

Carefully, I coached myself against the onslaught of want and temptation and gathered the clothes in my arms, intent to launder them so she could have them back and hopeful that the wait would be reason enough to keep her here.

"I'll be downstairs," I called over my shoulder as I exited the room.

I didn't wait to hear her response.

Frankly, I had a feeling it wasn't really something I'd want to hear anyway.

CHAPTER
TWELVE

Ivy

HIGH ON TIPTOE AND CONTORTING MYSELF TO COVER ALL OF THE things that counted, I danced around Levi's bathroom in search of a towel.

There weren't any in plain sight, and since the asshole had shoved me without permission into the fucking shower fully clothed, I'd had no choice but to strip down and wash away the cold of the rain.

Sure, the warmth of the water from his rain shower head had been soothing, and the steady pressure on my back had gone a long way to easing the ache the cold had created. But I didn't want to be trapped in his house, naked and vulnerable, while he took my clothes who knew where.

I was angry—depleted. So fucking tired of this back-and-forth between us that I felt like I'd been living it for years. We were two ships passing in the night, and when this was all over, we'd be miles in opposite directions.

There was absolutely no point in trying this hard. No point in torturing ourselves.

I sighed and shut my eyes as I let my own advice wash over me.

No point in *fighting*.

My shoulders sagged with the sudden loss of tension.

I need to let it all go.

Resolved to my new finding from my foray into self-discovery, I opened the cabinet under the sink and shut it, moved to the tall cabinet on the wall, and finally, found sanctuary in the form of a towel inside.

I wrapped the plush, navy blue fabric around myself and sank into the comfort of it, briefly inhaling the fresh laundry scent. It was indistinct, thankfully, rather than the linen embodiment of all things Levi Fox, so I gave myself over to the security it provided.

The shower and pep talk had taken me ninety percent of the way, but the fluffy gloriousness of the towel was the closer.

I was finally relaxed.

With fresh eyes and renewed interest, I surveyed the bathroom tile, a glossy white and gray swirl of marble, and the high-end fixtures, and I tried to find Levi in their opulence.

He was a cop in a small-town police department and basic in his needs from all accounts. He drove a beat-up truck and wore simple clothes, but this house—it was something else.

I moved then, cocooning myself in the towel as though it were a blanket, and exited the bathroom into the bedroom. It was big, if not ostentatious, and the ceiling was coffered.

Thought and detail had so obviously gone into the design of this home—most of it focused on looking grandiose. The more I saw, the more I felt like it was in competition with everything I knew about Levi.

But how well do you really know him?

The sarcastic, scorned part of me wanted to writhe around in the question and use it to build all of my walls back up, but for once, the practical part of me was louder.

I didn't know everything there was to know about Levi Fox.

Hell, I didn't even know a fraction of it.

But I *knew* this house didn't fit him.

As for why he lived in it despite the discrepancy, I had no clue.

Neat and tidy, a thick pile of clothes sat waiting on the edge of the bed. It'd clearly been arranged with care rather than being tossed mindlessly, and upon closer inspection, I discovered my phone, dried and wiped down, sitting next to it.

I picked it up and toyed with it, killing time while I fought with myself over whether to call Camilla or not.

She'd be wondering about my well-being, of that I was sure, but she'd also be forthright and overly pushy about what she thought the meaning of it all was. I wasn't really in the mood for a lecture.

Settling on middle ground, I shot her a quick text.

Me: I'm fine. Got caught in the rain and am drying out before heading home.

Camilla: Where are you drying out?

The little snooper. Couldn't let anything lie.

Me: I'll let you know when I'm on my way so you don't worry.

Camilla: ARE YOU AT LEVI'S??

Me: Bye.

Camilla: OMG, you are!! I knew it! But don't worry, I'll leave you alone about it.

The reprieve was surprising but not unwelcome. I was so *tired* of explaining myself.

Me: Thank you.

Camilla: For now. It'll be easier to beat it out of you in person.

Jesus. Great. Something to look forward to.

Me: You're so considerate.

Camilla: Of course I am. I'm the best. But what about Sam? Aren't you supposed to meet him for dinner tonight?

Me: I'll text him. Now leave me alone.

Camilla: Sure, sure. Get back to whatever you're doing. I'm sure it's interesting.

Me: I'm flipping you off right now.

Camilla: HAHA

Quickly backing out of Camilla's message thread before she could trap me with any more crap, I scrolled down to find Sam's name and opened his message. The last one, where we'd agreed to dinner tonight at El Loco, sat waiting at the top.

Me: Hey, Grandpa Sam. We're still on for dinner tonight, but I need a little extra time.

Sam: Sure, girl. You all right?

Me: Yeah, thanks. Just got caught in the rain. No big deal.

Sam: Caught in the rain? Rain don't melt ya, you know.

Me: I know. I was just out in it for a while and not at home. My clothes are drying.

Sam: Where in Sam Hill did you find a dryer?

Vague, Ivy. Be vague.

Me: I'm at a friend's house.

Sam: What friend? Last I checked, you had no friends here.

Gee, thanks. I considered my options for a minute before settling on the truth.

Me: Levi.

Sam: Uh-huh.

He didn't actually say anything, but there was a whole hell of a lot in his implication.

Me: Sam...it's not like that.

Sam: Sure, it ain't. How about we reschedule for tomorrow night?

Me: Tonight is fine. Just make it 8 instead of 7.

I waited for a full two minutes, but I didn't get anything back. I decided to assume that meant eight worked for him.

Done with talking to all of these annoying people, I tossed the phone on the bed, stripped off my towel Sherpa, and got down to the business of getting dressed.

Underwear, pajama pants, two layers of tops—all of it went on with ease.

It wasn't until I was fully encased, covered from head to foot, that I noticed.

These clothes, like the towel, were Levi's. But what the towel had lacked in personal affiliation, the clothes carried in spades.

They smelled bold and powerful and endlessly rich in a restrained mix of leather and citrus. I wasn't sure where he acquired those specific scents, as I'd never seen him in leather or holding fruit, but it was him all the same.

And considering I was inside his home, I wasn't likely to escape the olfactory web of Levi Fox anytime soon.

CHAPTER
THIRTEEN

Levi

MY POOL WAS CLOSED FOR THE WINTER, BUT IVY WAS SWIMMING all the same.

The sleeves of my sweatshirt hung from her arms like an old peasant dress, but the color was all it took to look right. The green set off the dark notes in her eyes and brought them to life in the center of her makeup-free face, and the collar of it moved in perfect synchronization with the auburn streaks of her wet hair.

She'd rolled up the legs of my pants to stop them from dragging and tied the drawstring at the waist as tight as it would go.

But maybe the most important of all, the fight had left her.

The storm clouds had moved on, and the sun was shining. And it was in the light that I suspected we'd find the truth.

She chewed at her bottom lip before stopping on the other side of the kitchen island. Hands covered by the overlong sleeves, she wiped at the surface mindlessly, staring at the motion of each hand for a long moment before meeting my eyes with her own.

"Thanks for the clothes."

I shrugged, letting just one corner of my mouth creep up from its resting position. "Sorry they're so big."

She lifted her eyebrow, just one smart remark she'd stopped

from escaping bleeding into the muscle.

"What?" I asked, wanting to know what had driven the skin higher. "What are you thinking?"

She shook her head and dragged her teeth across her lip. "It's just...I was thinking that they matched the house."

I glanced up immediately, surveying the over-tall cabinets and large, eat-in breakfast area. I knew the space was excessively spacious—I knew better than anyone. But I scarcely noticed it anymore. I didn't know that I even saw the place anymore. It was a place to go at night to sleep. That was it.

I allowed a self-deprecating laugh. "A little over the top, huh?"

She shrugged. "For someone else, maybe not. For you? Definitely."

"It was my dad's house," I told her, forcing myself to open up my life to her in a way I hadn't before.

She stared at me then, the silence stretching into the word she didn't say. *Was.* It was simple but specific, and I knew she had to be wondering at its use. I crossed the bridge and onto the next avenue of discussion for her.

"My dad died a few years ago, and my mom left when I was just a kid."

"She never came back?" Her question was soft. Knowing.

I shook my head.

"I'm sorry."

"Yeah, well...I can't blame her completely, I guess. Life with my dad was pretty shitty."

"Leaving her kid was shittier."

I shrugged, desperately not wanting to relive the story of young, motherless Levi, but I fought against the revolt. She deserved to know. If anything, she'd borne the brunt of this very hang-up.

"She, uh...she went to Hollywood. At least, that's the last I heard. I honestly couldn't tell you anything more than that, though."

"She never reached out?"

The shake of my head was slight. "No."

Her smile was sad but newly understanding. "No wonder you're not particularly fond of..." She paused and I waited, but in the end, she chose the innocuous noun. "Hollywood."

We both knew the word she was really after was "me."

I grinned and nodded, admitting, "Misdirected anger."

She sighed. "And I suppose you're just...*over* it now?"

I laughed. "I suspect not. But I'm trying."

And wasn't that the truth. I didn't have the tools to fix what I'd broken with Ivy, but I was trying my best to find them.

"I should probably get going."

I nodded even though the last fucking thing I wanted to do was nod. I wasn't ready for her to go. "Your clothes are in the dryer, but if you really need to go, you can take those, and I'll get yours back to you some other time."

Her hands disappeared into the depths of her hair as she pulled it back from her face. "I...yeah, just...I'll get them back from you. I'd wait for them, but I have to get ready for dinner."

My nod was jerky as I clamped my jaw shut.

Don't ask with whom. Don't ask with whom.

Her smirk was easy and mischievous. She knew I wanted to ask. "I *should* keep you in suspense."

"But?" I prompted.

Her smile grew, and my chest tightened. "But...it's with Grandpa Sam."

A war broke out just underneath my flesh. Grandpa Sam was a much better option than any of the others, but he was still Grace's family. I knew I was going to have to get over it—the invasion into Grace's life—but it wasn't something I could do on command.

She laughed humorlessly. "Good mood gone, huh?"

I ran an agitated hand over my face and sighed. There was no way I could go down this road without our nice conversation de-volving back into an argument.

Instead, I did something I didn't have much practice in—and let it go.

"Watch out for Sam. He's a major flirt."

She laughed, and her face melted into a surprised smile.

One point for me.

A coy eyebrow raised, she leaned into the counter and pulled up a sleeve teasingly. "He doesn't have to flirt. We're *already* an item."

A chuckle left my lips. It was rusty and highly unused, and if I wasn't mistaken, it had surprised the both of us.

"Maybe *he* sent you the flowers," I suggested, and her smile rat-cheted up ten notches.

"I'll have to ask him. But that's definitely something he would do."

I shrugged. "It's the kind of thing any good boyfriend would do."

Grace's face when I'd sent her flowers the first time flashed in my mind. It'd been so simple—a gesture I'd done for lack of coming up with one better. Friends for forever, I'd felt the necessity to distin-guish the difference between all that time and our first real date.

A delineation.

But to Grace, it'd meant everything.

"Yeah," Ivy said softly, bringing me back to the room with a startle. "I guess you're right."

She climbed off the barstool and walked slowly around the counter. I knew she was moments from walking out the door and rebuilding everything we'd managed to tear down, and I wasn't ready to let the easiness go.

"I'll walk you out."

"You don't have—"

"Ivy," I interrupted. "Just let me walk you out."

"All right," she conceded. "I just need my shoes."

My ears zeroed in on the tumbling thump of their presence in the dryer, and she followed the direction of my gaze.

"Huh," she muttered, catching on quickly. "I guess the gravel is going to hurt."

We walked to the door in silence. I used the time to stew on the statement, but I had no idea what she used it for. I figured, however, when she gasped as I swept her off her feet and into my arms outside the front door, that it hadn't been for the same thing.

"Levi!" she protested, but I ignored the complaints and walked all the way to her car.

She was light and, eventually, accommodating, which made it easy to open the car door and deposit her inside.

"I owe you thanks," she muttered. "Even though I didn't ask for the lift."

I smiled and shook my head. "Do you have to argue about everything?"

She grinned, asserting smartly, "Do *you*?"

The nondescript ring of my phone interrupted us. I pulled it from my pocket and glanced at the screen to find the chief's information displayed.

I put it to my ear without hesitation. "Chief?"

"Sam Murphy took a spill," he informed me without preamble. I started at the news, leaving uneasy eyes unchecked when they jumped to Ivy.

"What?" she asked, knowing that whatever I'd heard wasn't good news.

"They're taking him to the hospital now," the chief updated into my ear. "Thought you'd want to know."

"Thanks," I murmured as Ivy climbed to her feet, worry changing the brightness in her eyes to something unnaturally shiny.

"I'm calling Ivy next," he added, and my eyes locked with Ivy's now anxious gaze. "I guess they were supposed to go out to dinner."

"I'll tell her," I volunteered. "She's with me."

Hanging up instead of waiting for commentary from the chief that I probably had no interest in hearing, I gentled my voice and told Ivy the news. "Sam fell. They're taking him up to the hospital now, so dinner—"

She sat down in the car and slammed the door, not even waiting for me to finish the sentence.

The engine roared to life, and I had the good sense to step out of the way as she put the car in drive and pulled away.

"Goddammit, Ivy! Wait for me!" I yelled.

She sped out the driveway without looking back, so I headed for my truck at a dead run.

CHAPTER
FOURTEEN

Ivy

I WAS HALFWAY TO THE HOSPITAL BY THE TIME I REALIZED HOW ridiculous my reaction to the news had been.

Sam Murphy had come to mean a lot to me, but leaving Levi chasing after me in a spray of gravel was nearly ridiculous.

Sam wasn't my grandfather, and I wasn't Grace.

But the lines had so easily blurred.

When you spent all of your time trying to get into the mindset of someone else, training yourself to live their reactions, their thoughts, and their wants, it eventually took effect.

That was, frankly, the only explanation I had for the churn in my gut and the unsteady pooling in my eyes. I saw Sam Murphy as more than a friend—and it was because, at times, I could see myself as Grace.

I only wished I was smart as she'd been with her feelings around Levi.

Pulling into the parking lot on a screech of tires, I slid to a stop in a parking space near the emergency door and shoved the shifter into park.

Evidence and reason said I'd jump out of the car and haul ass inside, but the reality was different. Unsure and questioning my welcome, I sat still in the driver's seat of the silent car and gnawed at my lip.

Would Grace's family even want me here?

Would they see my arrival as an imposition?

Would I call unwanted attention to them?

I was still running the gamut of questions through my mind when a hard knock sounded on my window. I jumped at the unexpected noise and grasped at my chest, but the beating slowed to a reasonably normal pace when the hips bent and showed me a familiar set of blue eyes.

Levi didn't wait for me to roll down the window, instead, reaching for the door handle and pulling it open for me.

I didn't move from the seat, so he leaned down into the open V of the door and raised an eyebrow.

"You know…with the speed you used when leaving my house, I figured you'd be moving at at least a quarter of the pace when you got here."

I bit my lip and dropped my face into my hands, mumbling, "I'm not sure this was a good idea."

"What?" he asked. "Why the hell not?"

I jerked my face out of its cover, and the skin under my eyes pulled as I scrunched my nose. "Are you kidding? I'm not family. I care about Sam, so making sure he was okay was a knee-jerk reaction, but now that I'm here…I just…"

Levi squatted in the open space of the door, and the new position afforded me the opportunity to look directly into his eyes. They were open and surprisingly sympathetic given our history and how this all fit into it.

My chest squeezed, my subconscious poking at it to point out the change. But my brain didn't trust the validity or longevity of such a sharp swing. I followed the reasonable path and listened to my mind.

"Sam will be happy to see you. They all will. From what I've heard, the whole family has really taken a liking to you."

"From what you've heard?"

He rolled his eyes. "Yeah. Hard not to hear it." He smirked. "*Everyone* is talking about the *fabulous* Ivy Stone."

My voice dropped out, leaving nothing but the scraps at the bottom. "Everyone?"

He shook his head. "Not me."

My lips opened and closed, gulping for words like a fish. *Not him.*

He grabbed my chin and turned my face back up, back to a place where his eyes could easily capture mine. I fought the pull, but I was no match for his power in the end.

"Not me," he repeated like a fucking sadist.

I got it already.

He laughed at the rapidly degenerating look on my face and winked. "Not me, Ivy. But not because of you. It's not me talking because I don't *talk*."

He stood up suddenly and pulled me up with him, setting me on my sock feet on the cold pavement. The shock of the chill running through my feet and into my body pulled at my awareness.

"Oh my God," I screeched. "Look at what I'm wearing! I can't go in there like this!"

He ran his eyes up and down my body. He tried to hide it, but I couldn't have missed the way he smiled if he'd hidden it under a layer of concrete.

"Ugh," I whined. "Don't look at me like that. This isn't funny."

"Oh, yes, it is," he disagreed. "After weeks of seeing you in nothing but designer wear, this is funny."

"These are *your* clothes."

He smiled. "They don't look like *that* on me."

"Shut up!" I snapped, smacking him on the shoulder. "And I

haven't been wearing designer wear for weeks. I ordered new clothes when I got here."

He narrowed his eyes. "Still look pretty fancy to me."

"Obviously, I just wear them well."

He smirked, dragging his eyes over my appearance now once more. The bastard.

"I'm not going in there," I declared, my determination renewed. He shook his head.

"Yeah, you are. Come on."

I leaned back into the car, but his strength compared to mine was a joke. The body tug-of-war lasted all of a second.

"Levi! I don't want to go in!"

"Yes," he said, "you do. You're just too embarrassed about your goddamn clothes to admit it. But I can tell you right now, Sam Murphy doesn't give one shit about your outfit. He cares about a woman with a soft enough heart she would rush to the bedside of someone else's grandpa. Now get your ass moving before I move it for you."

Fearful of what he'd do if I didn't, I moved—sock feet and all.

■ ■ ■

"Oh my goodness, Ivy!" Mary Murphy gasped as she shot to her feet in the waiting room. "What's going on?" She looked down to my feet and worried her lip. "Are you okay?"

Embarrassment flushed my cheeks scarlet, and my tongue tied in a permanent knot.

Jesus. How the hell am I supposed to explain this outfit?

Levi spoke up from behind me. *Close* behind me.

"She got caught in the rain, Mary. I lent her some clothes."

"Oh," Mary said, getting the totally wrong idea. I rammed an elbow back, hoping desperately I was short enough to catch Levi where it really hurt.

He flinched, but I knew by the fact that he was still upright that I'd missed my target.

"I'm sorry I'm a mess," I apologized. "I just heard about Sam and couldn't stop myself from coming down to make sure he was all right."

"Oh, sweetie," Mary cooed, stepping forward to pull me under her arm lovingly. "He'll be happy to see you. He's doing fine, by the way. No broken bones so far, but they've got a few more scans to do."

I didn't look back as she pulled me away—I couldn't.

Something had broken the barrier between Levi and me tonight, and the more moments I spent with him, the more I worried I wouldn't be able to control myself or my heart for much longer.

CHAPTER
FIFTEEN

Levi

I GLANCED OUT IN THE HALL AT THE SOUND OF IVY'S LAUGH.

She was holding court with nearly half the damn town, her subpar outfit forgotten. She was made for the spotlight, and fame truly did become her. She put everyone around her at ease, and as much as I'd had trouble coming to terms with it in the beginning, her influence in Grace's family's life seemed genuinely positive.

They smiled and laughed and let go of some of their grief. They had faith in Ivy and the movie, and they wanted the closure for their loved one almost as much as they wanted it for themselves.

Just like me, they'd spent the last six years trying to get over it—but it'd taken the last few months to get them closer.

"She's somethin', huh?" Sam asked from my side, startling me with his presence. I'd damn near forgotten he was there, I'd been so entranced by watching Ivy.

"Who?" I asked, the innocent act sounding false to even my own ears.

Sam laughed outright. *"Who?* That's funny. Shoo!"

"Sam..."

"What, boy? You think I haven't noticed the way you look at her? The way she looks at you? I'm old, but my eyesight is just fine."

"It's complicated," I told him.

He laughed. "Yeah, Lee. I got that. But are you gonna tell me something I don't know?"

I shook my head with a smile and sat back in my chair. I tossed the tissue I'd been playing with for the last fifteen minutes in the garbage and turned his inquisition around on him. "Okay, big shot. Why don't you tell me? What should I be saying?"

Sam rolled his eyes and dove right into it, ornery righteousness thickening his normally crackly voice. "How about that you loved Grace, and while you kept your mouth shut about that for the sake of everyone else, it's been killing you every day since?"

The smile slipped off my face, but he kept going.

"Or you could talk about how you still feel guilty over what really happened to my granddaughter, and you've decided to close yourself off ever since?"

"Sam," I whispered, my voice tarnished. "How the hell—"

He waved an aggravated hand in front of his face. "Nobody else knows. But my granddaughter told me a lot of things, and with a little observation and a lot of time, I've put together the rest."

I closed my eyes and dropped my head back, covering my face with my hands.

"What I don't understand is why you're carrying any of that shit over to Ivy. You know as well as I do that she and Grace are two different people. About the only thing tying them together is you."

I uncovered my eyes and leaned into my knees. Sam met my eyes and held them.

"I'm not comparing the two of them." He scoffed, and I shook my head. "I'm not. Not anymore."

"Knock knock," Ivy said from the door. I spun my head quickly to her face, desperate to search it for signs that she'd heard what we were talking about.

A soft smile curved the corners of her lips and convinced me she hadn't caught even the tail end.

"I just wanted to say goodbye," she told Sam. "I'm gonna head home and get changed. But I'm glad you're doing okay. I'll be checking on you via text and bugging you until you're ready for a rain check on our dinner."

"Soon," he promised. "Mary will try to keep me bedridden, but they won't be able to keep me down."

Ivy laughed and turned to me. "Thanks, Levi," she muttered, confidence waning enough that she looked to the ground when she said my name. "I'll, uh, get these clothes back to you tomorrow at work. Maybe you can bring mine too?"

I nodded, but Sam caught my eye and glared, jerking his chin at Ivy. I did my best to give in to his demands.

"Ivy, wait," I called as she cleared the door to Sam's room and turned back at the sound of my voice.

"Yeah?"

"I'll walk you out."

This time, she didn't fight me.

"Okay."

■

Ivy was quiet as we walked side by side down the long hallway to the main entrance of the hospital.

It'd taken a few minutes to say our goodbyes, having to go through the bevy of Murphys and the chief and his wife, Margo, but we'd finally done it. Of course, I'd gotten a slap to the head from the chief as a parting gift.

As it turned out, he didn't like being hung up on, no matter the circumstances.

"Sorry for the way I took off," Ivy said, breaking in to the silence. "You know, back at your house. I realized on the way here how ridiculous it was."

I shrugged and gave her elbow a squeeze. "No big deal. And it wasn't ridiculous. It was nice to know you care about Sam that much. He seems to feel the same way about you."

"Were you talking about me in there?"

"Not really," I lied. "I can just tell."

Thankfully, she nodded, letting me off the hook instead of demanding an explanation.

The automatic doors at the entrance opened with a whoosh, and we stepped outside into the cold night air. The sun had set completely now, and any marginal warmth of the day had completely disappeared.

"God," she moaned as the bitter wave hit us in the face. "I don't know that I'll ever get used to the cold."

I smiled at that, thinking of how nice she must have it in California. Bad weather of slightly cloudy days and cold temperatures in the upper sixties. Born in raised in Cold, I only had my imagination to guide me.

"Must be a tough transition," I agreed, putting a soft hand to the small of her back as we headed for the car.

The windshields of every car we passed were foggy with the change in temperature, but when hers came into view, I pulled her to a stop with a fierce grip on the fabric of her sweatshirt.

My bones locked, and my lungs froze as the past washed over me.

On her windshield, smudged into the frosty glass, was a distinctly familiar broken heart.

CHAPTER
SIXTEEN

Ivy

LEVI STOPPED DEAD IN HIS TRACKS, HIS STRONG HAND WRAPPED around the material of my sweatshirt and preventing me from moving any closer to the car.

I followed his gaze to the windshield of my rental.

Oh my God. I gasped and lifted my hand to cover my mouth while my brain tried to make sense of it all.

I blinked. Once. Twice. Three times.

As I stared at the plate of clear glass, my gaze took in the familiar shape of a tiny broken heart drawn into the frost.

Nearly a replica, it mirrored the tiny broken heart Walter Gaskins had carved into his victims' skin.

Morbid and vile thoughts filled my head, and I shuddered.

Surely, it was just a tasteless joke by someone with way too much time on their hands.

It had to be a prank...*right?*

I didn't know the answer, but I knew whoever had done this was the biggest, most disgusting, thoughtless asshole I'd ever had the unfortunate—*the exact opposite of pleasure*—of knowing existed.

Two steps forward and my hand trembled as I slid a damp, folded piece of paper out from its place nestled beneath one of the windshield wipers.

Like a faucet opened up to full capacity, adrenaline spilled into my veins, and both of my hands trembled as I unfolded the note.

The black ink was smeared down the page in ominous drips and drops, likely from the moisture in the air. With a shaky inhale, I scrolled over the words, and once I came to the signature, I dropped the sheet of paper like it had lit up in flames.

"What?" Levi questioned. "What does it say?"

I didn't have a response, my brain too muddled with confusion and fear.

He leaned down and lifted the now even wetter paper from the ground with just his fingertips and read it, the menacing words falling from his lips in hushed and concern-filled waves. "*Notice this. Notice me. Notice everything I send to you. Love, Me.*"

Me.

Only two letters. One tiny little word. But it packed a hellish punch. Straight to my gut, that single word held the power to make me want to fall to my knees.

"The flowers you got at Grace's house," Levi said, breaking the deafening silence. His eyes moved slowly from the sheet of paper and didn't stop until they locked with mine. "The card was signed the same way?"

"Yes."

"Does the handwriting look familiar?"

"The card for the flowers was pre-printed."

"*Fuck,*" he muttered and ran a frustrated hand through his already messy dark locks. "We shouldn't have touched this note. This should've been treated like a crime scene."

"A crime scene?" I asked, and my eyes popped wide in confusion.

"Yes," Levi responded without hesitation. "A fucking crime scene, Ivy. Those flowers, this note, that fucking broken heart drawn onto your windshield. This is *not* okay."

"You can't arrest someone for writing me a note or sending me flowers, Levi."

"Yeah, but I can make sure we have evidence on hand if shit like this continues to escalate."

"Escalate?" I damn near shouted.

Holy fucking shit. I wasn't sure I liked the sound of that.

And…escalate to what?

Pretty sure you do not want to start thinking about worst-case scenarios right now…

Nausea roiled and coiled itself inside of my stomach as Levi placed a strong hand on the small of my back and led me the few steps toward his truck.

I didn't question or pull away, though. I was too damn focused on not letting my brain veer down a path where I had racing thoughts about a psychopath kidnapping and killing me.

He unlocked his vehicle and opened the back passenger's-side door with a quick jerk of his wrist. After rummaging in the back for a good twenty seconds, he pulled a container of clear Ziploc bags from a black duffle with the words COLD PD inscribed on the side.

Carefully, he released the note from his fingertips and slid it inside an empty plastic bag and secured it closed.

"W-what are you doing?" I asked once my brain caught up with the fact that he was wrapping up the note like you would a turkey sandwich.

"Evidence," he said and placed the bag inside his duffle before zipping it closed. "We can test that fucking note for fingerprints. Do you still have the card from the flowers?"

I shrugged. "I'm not sure. I don't really remember what I did with it, to be honest."

"No doubt, both items will already be riddled with your fingerprints and mine, but maybe the crime lab can find someone else's DNA on them."

"Levi," I said on a deep sigh. "This is crazy. I agree that the note and the…" I paused, unable to form the words to describe that tiny little heart. "The…the windshield were in poor taste. But no one committed a crime."

He popped open the passenger door and nodded toward the interior. "Get in."

"What?" I questioned.

"You're staying with me tonight," he answered.

With a hand to my hip, I offered my retort without delay. "Uh… no, I'm not."

He sighed, heavy, deep, and I could tell it was his exasperated sigh. The one that only left his lungs when he was really at his wit's end. "Yes. You. Are."

"This makes no sense."

"The fact that you're not realizing how very serious this might be makes no sense," he interjected. "Ivy, I can't let you sleep at Grace's house tonight, or any other night, for that matter. Tomorrow you can work on finding another house to rent for the duration of filming."

I stared at him, and he stared back at me. His midnight-blue eyes were so damn resolute.

"This feels a little overboard, Levi."

"Trust me," he responded. "This isn't overboard. This is exactly how we need to handle this."

We, he'd said. Like we were some sort of team. Like we were together.

"Just get in the car, Ivy." His voice stretched thin with patience. "It's either you get in the truck, or I will put you in the truck."

I rolled my eyes. "Caveman, much?'

He just shrugged. "I'll do whatever I have to do to keep you safe. If that means being a caveman, then so be it. Bring on the loincloths, animal hides, and wooden clubs. I'm game."

"You're infuriating, you know that?"

Another fucking shrug, only this time, a smirk followed it. "I can say the same about you, sweetheart."

"What about my rental?" I asked, nodding toward the now defaced car.

"I'll call the station and have someone come by to pick it up."

"And what about clothes? And Camilla? I can't leave my sister there to fend for herself."

"I already planned on her staying at my place too. We'll head on over to Grace's old house now, and you can call your sister on the way and explain the situation. Surely, she'll understand," he responded in a far-too-knowing voice.

Fucking hell, he is right.

Camilla would lose her shit when I told her. And, considering the fact that before I'd left LA to come to Cold, I'd had a bit of a stalker situation on my hands, she had every right to.

My twin would start packing up our stuff the moment I let her know about the creepy broken heart finger-painted onto the windshield.

"Now, get your little ass in the truck and let me keep you and your sister out of harm's way. Okay?"

What could I do?

He had a point. I doubted I could sleep at Grace's house even if I had the option. And more than that, I couldn't risk my sister sleeping there either.

Whoever was sending me all of this weird shit obviously had the address.

And apparently, they also knew what car I drove.

It was alarming. And scary. And, if I was being honest, I was thankful Levi was here.

He hadn't hesitated to take charge of the situation.

And to protect you.

Once my ass was in the passenger seat, Levi shut the door and walked around the front of the truck.

As soon as our tires hit the road, he put a call out to the station and let them know the situation, while I sent Camilla a quick text.

Me: Hey, so, we need to stay somewhere else tonight. Can you start packing an overnight bag for us? I'll be there in about 10 minutes.

Camilla: Huh?

Me: There's been a bit of a situation, and we won't be able to stay in Grace's house anymore. Levi and I are headed to the house now. Just pack up the essentials for tonight, and we'll work on getting everything else tomorrow.

Camilla: Situation? I'm so confused right now...

Me: I'll explain everything when I get there. Be there in about 10 minutes.

Me: Oh, and keep the doors locked.

Shit. I probably shouldn't have sent that, but I couldn't help myself.

If anything happened to Camilla, I didn't know what I'd do.

Camilla: Keep the doors locked??? Should I be worried?

Yeah. Definitely shouldn't have sent that.

Me: No. Just cautious. I promise everything is fine. And I'll explain it all when I get there.

Camilla: Where are we staying tonight?

Me: Levi's.

Camilla: Oh, man. You're just tossing out plot twists everywhere, huh? And now, I'd say it's pretty obvious you have SO much to tell me. But don't worry, I'll make sure that happens very, very soon.

No doubt, I would receive the sister inquisition tonight. I couldn't blame her, though. I'd be doing the same thing if I were in her shoes.

Me: Jesus. Just pack us an overnight bag, okay?

Camilla: Uh-huh... ;) Consider it done. But prepare yourself, the interrogation is near...

Me: (insert heavy sigh) I'm well aware.

■

"Did you get Ivy's rental?" Levi asked as he took a right out of Grace's driveway and headed toward the main road.

"Dane is bringing it back to the station now." Officer Glen Chase's voice filtered in through the Bluetooth speakers of Levi's truck. "You headed home now?"

"Yeah," Levi responded. "Both Ivy and Camilla are going to stay with me for the night."

"Good idea," Glen responded.

While Levi proceeded to give Glen a rundown of things he wanted done, my phone pinged with a text message notification, and I pulled it out of my purse only to find that my sister, who was currently sitting in the back seat of Levi's truck, was texting me.

COLD

Camilla: Where are you going to sleep tonight?

My nose scrunched up in confusion.

Me: Uh...the same place you're going to sleep.

Camilla: You know that's not what I meant.

Me: Are you being serious right now?

Camilla: Uh-huh. :)

Me: I will be sleeping in a guest room. By myself.

Camilla: That's lame.

Me: You're lame.

Camilla: Also, I'm a little pissed you didn't tell me about Officer Dane Marx.

Me: Dane? How do you know Dane?

Camilla: I met him this afternoon while you were otherwise occupied.

Me: Met him where?

Camilla: I had to make a grocery run. I ran out of French vanilla creamer, and you know I cannot start my day without it in my coffee.

Me: You met Dane at the grocery store?

Camilla: Yep. And he is fucking adorable.

Me: Well, well, well...looks like I'm not the only one who deserves a sister interrogation.

Camilla: Oh, stop it. There's not much to tell.

Me: Interesting that you're bringing him up, though...

Camilla: Yeah. I'm ignoring you now.

I silently giggled at her response and decided to let the subject go for a little while.

Well, at least until we got to Levi's house and I could ask her a million questions without having to use our phones as a third party.

I wanted to ask questions and actually *see* her reactions.

It was easy for her to hide behind a device, but in person, she had a hell of a time hiding her true feelings.

Relief settled into my veins over the fact that Levi, Camilla, and I were all inside of his truck, heading toward his house where we'd all cohabitate for the night, and even after everything that had happened, it wasn't awkward.

Weirdly enough, it just felt normal. It felt right.

Levi's phone conversation with Glen was long done, and I took it upon myself to adjust the volume knob for the stereo until music filled the otherwise silent cab of his truck.

I switched through the channels until I found an oldies station playing Ben E. King.

The last few beats of "Stand by Me" reverberated through the speakers, and I settled into the passenger seat as Levi took a left turn on a snow- and dirt-covered back road.

Out of my periphery, I glanced at him, taking in the edges of his strong jaw, the way his jet-black hair looked even darker beneath the night sky, and the way his dark blue gaze stayed focused on the road.

He was handsome, painfully so, and that I couldn't deny.

Through the passenger window, I looked out across the miles and miles of pristine and white-covered plains of Montana. The snowcapped mountains provided a majestic background, and the moon bouncing off the snow only made the landscape more beautiful.

The song switched over, and Roy Orbison started singing about being lonesome and Blue Bayou.

I sighed, soft and slow. A memory from my childhood, I could remember my dad playing this very song on an old record player that, to this day, he still refused to get rid of.

Levi muttered something under his breath, and I darted my eyes from the window until they met the now harsh, pained lines of his jaw.

"Fuck. Not today. Of all fucking days," he mumbled, more to himself than anyone else in the truck, and with a quick tap of his index finger, slid the knob to the off position and sent us into silence.

"You don't like Roy Orbison?" I asked, and he only offered a short shake of his head and a curt two-word response.

"Not anymore."

I didn't have a response to that. But my brain was trying its damnedest to decode the secret messages only Levi appeared to know and understand.

He glanced at me out of the corner of his blue eyes as he pulled into the driveway of the veritable mansion he called home.

With a twist of his wrist, he turned off the engine and Camilla opened the back passenger door of the crew cab and hopped out.

But Levi grabbed my wrist before I could follow her lead.

"It's a long story," he said, and our gazes locked.

I scrunched up my nose, and he nodded toward the radio.

"The song, I mean," he said. "It's a long story, but one day soon, I'll tell you all about it. But today is just not that day. We've already had too much shit to face as it is."

I'll tell you all about it.

The vulnerability in those words pushed against my heart, and it responded by increasing its tempo and making its presence known inside my chest.

He never wanted to tell me anything.

Until now.

I searched his eyes, expecting the familiar closed-off reaction I'd received so many times before, but staring back at me was a man who wasn't holding anything back or trying to keep secrets. His midnight-blue eyes were merely asking for some time and patience.

"Okay," I whispered back.

CHAPTER
SEVENTEEN

Levi

THOUGHT IT WAS HALF-PAST ELEVEN BY THE TIME WE'D ARRIVED AT my house, Ivy and Camilla had already managed to make themselves comfortable and settle into the spare guest rooms of my house.

Surely, I had enough room.

We probably could've brought another four guests, and the house still wouldn't have been filled.

I'd lain awake for the past hour or so, trying not to eavesdrop on their conversation, but despite how quiet they were trying to be, their voices carried through the otherwise silent rooms and hallways with ease.

"So, what happened?"

Instantly, I knew that voice was Camilla.

Although the sisters were identical, near replicas of each other in every physical attribute, their voices, their tones, the way they pushed their words past their lips had distinctive differences.

Where Camilla was generally more soft-spoken, her words a low hum or a lull, Ivy was all rasp, and her voice carried, even when she was trying to whisper.

"Nothing," Ivy responded quietly.

"Oh, come on," her sister answered, amusement and annoyance highlighting the edges of her voice. "You ended up at his house earlier today. You were late to dinner with Sam because you were here. And, to top it all off, you were together when you came and picked me up from the house."

"Well, technically, Sam and I didn't meet up for dinner," Ivy responded. "He had a fall and ended up in the hospital."

"Oh my God!" Camilla gasped. "Is he okay?"

"Yeah. He's fine. Both Levi and I went to visit him before we... well...before we picked you up."

"So, you basically spent the whole day with him?" Camilla questioned.

Ivy didn't respond, but that apparently didn't stop Camilla from continuing the conversation.

"You know you can tell me anything, Ivy," she said. "I feel like you're not wanting to tell me because you think I still have some misplaced feelings for him. I also think you're forgetting the fact that the only reason I kissed him in the first place was because I had no idea something had been going on between the two of you. If you'd actually given me a heads-up, I never would have made a move."

"Do you have feelings for him?" Ivy asked.

"I'm not going to deny I was interested in him, but to say I had feelings would be a pretty big fucking stretch," she responded with a giggle. "I'd just met him. And sure, he was sweet to me in the beginning and had shown me some attention, but I wasn't, like, planning our marriage and shit. To me, he would've just been someone to fill the time with while we were stuck in this godforsaken frozen tundra."

A soft laugh reverberated down the hall, and I knew it was Ivy's.

"I'm sorry I didn't tell you from the beginning about Levi. I was just confused. We fought...a lot. Then, between all that fighting, we'd kiss. And it...well...I didn't know what the fuck was going on.

He's not exactly the easiest egg to crack. If anything, he's the exact type of man I should avoid."

Straight to the chest, her words, the ones I knew I wasn't supposed to hear, hit me hard.

And, God, it stung like a motherfucker.

But I couldn't deny that what she'd said was true.

With the way I'd been from the very first day she'd arrived in Cold, I was the exact kind of man Ivy Stone should avoid.

But I didn't want to be that kind of man anymore. I wanted to be the man Ivy would run toward with open arms. The kind of man she could trust and rely on. Someone who only made her feel good and safe and fucking happy.

"Today"—Ivy's voice filled my ears—"I went to his house to return the flowers I'd thought he'd sent me. And, well, I ended up throwing them at him, and then, we did what we always do. We fought…a lot. Then, we kissed."

"Jesus. I'm disappointed in myself for not catching on to all the sexual-tension vibes flowing between the two of you."

"We do not—"

"Shut up." Camilla laughed. "Don't bullshit me, you little bullshitter. You two are attracted to each other like fucking magnets. And you know what I think?"

"What do you think?"

"I think you need to just give in to it and fuck his brains out."

"Cami!" Ivy shouted on a whisper-yell.

"Oh, come on," Camilla retorted. "You know you're curious. You know you want to. I think you need to just give in to all the pent-up sexual tension and have some goddamn fun."

"That's an awful plan."

"But is it? I mean, really?" Camilla questioned.

"Well, considering everything that's happened, I'm not sure it's the best plan."

"You mean everything that's happened in the past?" her sister questioned. "Ivy, sometimes, you just have to let go of the past. Sometimes, people make mistakes, but that doesn't make them bad people. And, from what I've seen, Levi Fox has been trying to make some serious amends for his sins."

Silence stretched between them for a few quiet moments, until Camilla spoke up again. "You're single. You haven't had *that* kind of fun in a long fucking time. I think it's time, honey. Between your crazy work schedule and all of the other bullshit that comes along with being one of Hollywood's sweethearts, you deserve a little fun."

"And what about you?" Ivy asked. "Your work schedule is just as crazy as mine."

"That's exactly why I'm going to make damn sure I have some fun while we're spending our days and nights in the fucking arctic."

"Is this where Dane Marx comes in?"

"He's definitely on my list of fun possibilities."

Ivy giggled. "I love you, you know that?"

"I love you too. Now, get the hell out of my room and go get some sleep. We've got an early day tomorrow."

More giggles and soft laughter filled the house until a bedroom door opened and shut.

As what I assumed were the sounds of Ivy's soft footsteps moving across the hardwood floor of the hallway reached my ears, I turned over on my side and adjusted the pillow underneath my head until I found the most comfortable position.

Another bedroom door opened and closed.

Eventually, all that was left was utter silence.

I let my eyes fall closed, and for once, I felt like sleep might come easy tonight.

■

A turn of a knob, the creak of the door, the sounds filled the space of my bedroom, and I opened my eyes, searching the darkened space for a visitor.

Softly, footsteps moved toward me, and I sat up in bed to find a petite figure approaching me.

"Ivy?"

"Yes... Wait—" She paused, her voice and her steps. "Oh my God, are you *checking* to make sure you know which sister I am?"

Of course I wasn't fucking checking.

Even though Ivy and her sister were identical twins, and it was the middle of the fucking night, I knew the difference by now. Where Camilla would be careful with her steps and her movements, Ivy was the type of woman who walked into a room and made damn sure you knew she was there, even when she was attempting to be quiet.

I nearly wanted to laugh at her accusation, but instead, I decided to roll with it.

"Would you rather I *didn't* check?" I asked sarcastically.

"Are you fucking serious, Levi?" she spat out on a whisper.

"Now, calm down for a second," I muttered and pushed the sheets off my body to free my legs. I moved them until they hung off the edge of the bed and my back was vertical. "It's late. I'm half asleep. And there are literally no lights on. So, please, give me a break here. I wasn't trying to be an asshole."

"Kind of seemed like it." She huffed out a sigh, and my gaze adjusted to the darkness until I could really see her. Ivy stood before me, dressed in her version of pajamas—silky and soft and leaving little to the imagination.

Fucking hell.

The light of the moon shone in through the windows of my bedroom and only added to her beauty.

"Is everything okay?" I asked, and she just shrugged. "Do you need something?"

Say me. Say you need me.

She shrugged again.

I couldn't not laugh at the irony of the situation. She'd made her way into my bedroom in the middle of the night, but she appeared hesitant to tell me why.

"Don't laugh at me."

I raised both hands in the air. "I swear I'm not laughing at you."

A hand to her little hip, she tapped a determined foot against the ground. "You're a horrible liar, Levi Fox."

I patted the spot on the bed beside me, but she didn't budge.

I patted it again. "I don't bite. Promise."

Another sigh. A few more taps of her foot. But, eventually, she moved toward me and sat down. Vanilla and silk and a scent that could only be Ivy hit me like a freight train.

Everything about this woman called to me, even the way she fucking smelled.

"The song," she whispered, but her eyes didn't meet mine. She stared down at her fingers that were now fidgeting in her lap. "Why don't you like that song?"

"Is that why you came in here?" I asked, and she just shrugged... *again*.

"I'm just curious. And you said..." She paused and lifted her gaze to mine. "You said you'd tell me."

Ivy deserved my truth. And even though a large part of me just didn't want to discuss the very subject she was trying to broach, I knew I'd never gain her trust without being willing to push through my own discomfort, my own hang-ups, my fucking past that I'd let haunt me for far too long.

I inhaled a long, slow breath and let out the air on a cleansing sigh. "That was the song that was playing when..." I paused for a brief moment, until I found the strength to explain. "'Blue Bayou' was the song Walter Gaskins had playing inside his house when Grace died. That fucking song was what filled my ears as she took her last breath."

Ivy's eyes widened and her lips parted, and without hesitation, she reached out and placed her hand in mine. "God...that's horrible," she whispered.

"Yeah," I whispered back. "It was his song, apparently. The one he played when he was..." I paused, not because I couldn't say the words, but because I didn't think Ivy actually needed the words. My silence was answer enough.

She stayed quiet, and her gaze searched mine for a long moment.

"I don't like that song anymore either," she said, and for some odd reason, it urged the corners of my mouth to lift up ever so slightly.

All at once, with her emerald eyes staring into mine, she hit me like a ray of sun. Everything I needed and more was written all over her. An angel beneath the soft glow of the moon, she might as well have had a fucking golden halo hanging over her head.

I swore I'd never fall again.

But this wasn't even falling.

This was being awakened.

All of those walls I'd built, I watched as they tumbled from around my soul and hit the ground in a rubble of dust and dirt.

Every rule I'd had, she'd broken.

Every promise I'd made to myself, she'd forced me to reconsider.

Before Ivy, I hadn't wanted any risks.

But now, I'd take every fucking risk if it meant being with her.

I'd risk it all.

Without thinking or second-guessing, I did the one thing I'd been dying to do.

I slid my fingers into the soft and silky locks of her hair and pressed my lips to hers. She responded with fervor, her full lips moving against mine in a rough and unsteady rhythm.

Our kiss grew deeper and deeper until her arms were wrapped around my neck, and I pulled her into my lap, her thighs straddling my hips.

God, she felt so good. Tasted so good. Everything I'd been imagining for the past several weeks did not live up to the real thing.

I needed her. This. Us.

I needed to taste her. Touch her. Feel her.

I needed to be inside of her.

I wanted to mark her as mine. Claim her. Show her that she belonged to me.

Because she did.

Ivy Stone belonged to me.

And I belonged to her too.

CHAPTER
EIGHTEEN

Ivy

"**N**OW. *NOW*," I MOANED AGAINST HIS LIPS.

I needed him. The cravings for him ran so deep within my veins I wouldn't be able to leave this room until I'd felt him inside of me. Until I'd heard his moans. Felt his groans against my lips. And watched his eyes glaze over as he filled me up.

Between one breath and the next, he had my pajama shorts and panties off and tossed to the floor.

Impatient, I reached up and pulled him down, his body hovering over mine as he removed his boxer briefs and threw them across the room.

My thighs shook, and needy moans spilled from my lips as I anticipated what he would feel like. Impatient and greedy, I waited with bated breath for him to slide his cock inside of me.

But he wasn't being fast enough.

"Fuck me," I whispered, and my eyes pleaded with his.

He didn't speed up, didn't race to the proverbial finish line that ended with us fucking. He just stared down at me, midnight-blue eyes even darker and deeper in intensity beneath the soft glow of the moon filtering in through the bedroom windows.

Slow, oh so very slow, he leaned forward and pressed his lips to my neck. He suckled tenderly against the sensitive skin, his tongue running along my thrumming pulse, until those lips of his turned hungry and placed greedy, openmouthed kisses along my neck, across my collarbone, and down my chest.

I moaned, and my eyes fell closed.

As his body moved down mine, his lips dropping kisses on every inch of my skin, his cock brushed against me, *there, right there,* in that oh so perfect place where I throbbed and ached for him.

My hips moved of their own accord, my body too high on desire and only responding on instinct.

I wanted his cock inside of me. So bad. So fucking bad.

"Please," I whispered. "Now, Levi."

But my words didn't have any effect.

He didn't speed up or slow down; he just continued what he was doing, his warm breath and hot mouth worshiping my skin.

When his lips found my breast, I trembled.

And when the tip of his tongue circled my nipple, goose bumps pebbled my skin and tiny little jolts of pleasure rolled along my spine, running all the way down my legs and making my toes curl.

His lips were on my belly now, and between sensual kisses, those intense eyes of his locked with mine. "I feel like I've been waiting three lifetimes to do this. To see you like this," he whispered just below my belly button, and his big, strong hands gripped my thighs, spreading them even farther.

I whimpered.

"Your beauty wrecks me, Ivy."

"Please," I begged. "Fuck me, Levi."

Ever so slightly, he shook his head. "I'm not fucking you tonight."

"You're not?" I asked on a whisper, my eyes growing wide in confusion.

"No, I'm not," he responded. "This is way more than just fucking."

But he didn't give me any time to process those words. Kneeling between my thighs and gripping his cock with one hand, he guided himself to where I was wet and hot and needy for him.

I watched in rapt attention as he pushed himself inside of me, inch by inch by inch, and oh so fucking slow.

Time might as well have stood still in that moment.

There was nothing rushed or impulsive about this.

When his big, thick cock filled me up completely, a raw, guttural moan spilled from my lips.

God, he felt so good.

So right.

"More," I said, my voice a mere whimper, my brain too delirious with want and need and pleasure. "Please, more."

Still on his knees, still oh so deep inside of me, he reached forward and pulled me onto his lap.

"Wrap your hands around my neck," he whispered, and I listened.

Nose-to-nose, chest-to-chest, we stared at one another. Our gazes locked in a maelstrom of desire and need and something else that felt too strong to confront.

Slow and purposeful, he gripped my hips with his big hands as he guided me up and down his hard length.

Up and down.

Up and down.

He savored every small, tiny thrust by kissing me deeply.

He moaned when he picked up the pace, going faster and deeper and increasing the intensity.

But the entire time, one thing never changed.

He looked at me. Not my breasts. Or my pussy. Or the way my body was wrapped around him like a second skin.

But into my eyes. My soul. Into my heart.

He looked at *me*.

I searched his eyes for the meaning. And when I'd found the slightest inkling of what I'd been looking for, my heart rate kicked up, tripping into a fast, erratic rhythm.

It was too much. He was too much.

It was too good. He felt too right.

Vulnerable and scared I'd just up and hand him my heart, I averted my eyes.

But he didn't let me avoid him…this…*us.*

With a gentle finger underneath my chin, he reoriented my face so that our gazes were locked again, tied together by some invisible string.

"Give me your eyes," he whispered and laid us back on the bed.

He pushed himself deep again, and my eyes drifted closed, a moan escaping my lips.

"Never stop giving me those eyes, Ivy," he said as he rested his elbows beside my head.

Pleasure and desire taking over, he picked up the pace, his cock driving in and out of me in heavy strokes.

I felt like I would unravel at the seams. Like I would explode into a million tiny pieces. I gripped his shoulders with my hands, my nails pushing into his skin, as I tried to hold myself together.

But it was no use. He held all the power in this.

And he knew my body better than I did.

"Give me your lips."

"Give me your tongue."

"Give me your pleasure."

Give me. Give me. Give me.

My brain wanted to defy him.

My heart wanted to give him everything.

Levi knew when to be soft and when to be hard.

He knew just how to kiss my neck and breathe into my ear and caress my sensitive, aching skin with his fingertips.

He knew just how to move his cock inside of me, going deep, going slow, going fast, but always hitting the right spots to make me beg for more.

All the while, the pleasure was building inside of me.

His kisses turned long and profound, and I gasped from the feel of him, the taste of him, from...*him.*

Bodies entwined and Levi whispering my name, I felt the instant my heart decided.

I felt the instant it reached out of my chest and fused with his.

I had no control over it.

I had no say in the matter.

It just was.

Like it always had been.

The push and pull between us, the fighting, the screaming, the awful things we'd done and said to one another...my heart didn't care about any of it.

It only felt.

It only wanted one person.

Levi.

When the need to chase my pleasure grew too strong, I gave in. I let my body feel it all. Each thrust. Each kiss. Each touch.

I didn't hold back.

I didn't think about anything else.

Just him.

Just us.

Just right now.

My heart pounded erratically, and my breaths came out in unsteady pants as I rose higher and higher and higher.

And with my body entwined with his, green eyes staring into blue, I gave him my pleasure, coming hard around his cock.

My body shook and trembled, and moans spilled from my lips as he followed my lead.

His back grew rigid, and his hands clenched the sheets on the bed as he pushed himself as far as he could go, spilling himself inside of me.

Sated and limp, he lay down beside me and pulled me on top of his big, muscular body.

My head resting against his chest, I felt each inhale and exhale of his lungs and each thump-thump of his heart. And I let those sounds of his soothe me until I felt my eyes grow heavy with sleep.

CHAPTER
NINETEEN

Levi

THE FIRST ANNOYING BLEEPS OF MY ALARM STARTLED ME AWAKE, and with my eyes still closed, I felt across the bed blindly until I reached my phone on the nightstand.

Slowly and reluctantly, I uncovered my face from beneath the sheets.

I blinked, closed my eyes, and blinked again until I gained the sight needed to turn the goddamn alarm off before it dove into round two of its personal rendition of *sounds from hell*.

Streaks of sunlight penetrated the window and damn near blinded me as I worked to focus and steady my groggy gaze.

Like a waterfall, a rush of thoughts and memories, all revolving around last night, flooded my mind.

Ivy.

Ivy *and* me. Together. Entangled. *Connected*.

I'd kissed, caressed, worshiped every inch of her body.

I'd been so deep inside of her I hadn't known where I ended and she began.

I'd swallowed her moans, felt her clench around my cock as she came all over me.

I'd memorized every inch of her body. Every sound. Every taste.

You made love to her last night.

I looked to my right, only to find the space her perfect body once filled completely empty.

Dread and disappointment filled my gut.

I couldn't deny her lack of presence *affected* me.

I'd fallen asleep last night with Ivy in my arms, looking forward to waking up that very same way, but she was nowhere to be found.

I listened closely for the sounds of the master bathroom, but nothing.

My gaze scanned across the floor of my bedroom, searching for remnants of her presence last night, but not a single item remained. Not her silk pajamas or lace panties. Nothing.

Shoving the sheets and comforter off my body, I dragged my feet out of bed, sat up on the side of the mattress, and rubbed my knuckles over my eyes.

I had no idea where Ivy went, but I could only assume both she and Camilla were getting ready for another day on set.

Because of daylight and landscape preferences for all outdoor scenes, Hugo Roman had the entire cast and crew starting their day at nine this week.

Standing and stretching out the creaks and kinks of my muscles, I slid on my boxer briefs and headed into the master bathroom.

The soft sounds of voices filtered up from downstairs, and a small sense of relief fluttered inside my stomach.

She was still here.

I'd like to say I'd planned on taking a shower and starting my day with my normal routine, but that would've been a lie.

I needed to see her. Talk to her. Find out why I'd woken up alone.

A few minutes later, dressed in a pair of gray sweat pants and a white T-shirt, I jogged down the stairs to the main floor.

Ivy stood at the kitchen island while Camilla sat on one of the barstools across from her, staring down at the screen of her phone.

"Morning," I greeted, and Camilla's gaze lifted to mine.

"Good morning, Levi," she responded, eyes friendly.

But, Ivy… She only offered a barely mumbled, "Hey."

They were both dressed and ready to start their day.

"Hungry?" I asked.

"I stole a granola bar from the pantry," Camilla answered, her smile half apologetic and half mischievous. "Hope you don't mind."

I grinned. "Not at all. Feel free to help yourself to anything."

My gaze moved to Ivy, who still stood at the kitchen island, her hip resting against the edge. "Did you eat something? I can make you some eggs," I offered, knowing it was part of her normal routine.

She shook her head. "I'm not hungry."

"What about some coffee?" I asked, and she shook her head again.

"No, thanks."

Wow. If her warmth toward me had a degree, it'd be fucking frigid.

But before I could say anything else, three heavy knocks to the front door filled the otherwise silent space between the three of us.

"Oh!" Camilla exclaimed and hopped out of her seat. "That's probably Dane."

She was out of the kitchen and headed for the foyer between one breath and the next, Ivy following her lead.

What in the fuck is going on?

Reeling over Ivy's suddenly closed-off demeanor, I stood frozen in my spot by the coffee machine for a few quiet moments, but once Dane's deep chuckle filled my ears, I knew I needed to head toward the front door and greet him.

The three of them stood inside the open foyer, and the small overnight bags the girls had packed were in Dane's hands.

"Mornin', Levi," he greeted with an overzealous grin, his body clad in his Cold PD uniform.

I nodded. "What brings you here this early?"

"Well," he started, and I didn't miss the fact that his gaze averted toward a bright-eyed Camilla. "Cam called me about an hour ago and asked me to bring their rental car here."

"Oh, okay," I muttered, and my eyes locked with Ivy's for the briefest of moments.

But she gave nothing in return. Her lips remained in a firm line, and her emerald eyes were so damn cold they were nearly blue.

"Thank you so much for letting us stay here last night, Levi," Camilla chimed in.

"Anytime," I responded, but my gaze stayed fixated on Ivy. "And there's no rush. You can both stay here until you find another place to rent."

"I already found us something," Ivy updated, but her eyes never met mine. "Production pulled some quick strings and found us another rental."

"That's…good to hear."

"Yeah. It is." Her gaze flitted to mine, but the connection didn't last for more than a fucking second or two. "Thanks for letting us stay here last night."

I just nodded in return. I mean, what else could I do? My mind was one hundred versions of fucked-up, trying to figure out the meaning behind her abrupt, cold-as-ice behavior.

"All right!" Camilla exclaimed and started to move for the door. "Well, we better get a move on it. Dane, do you mind dropping me off at our new digs so Ivy can drive the rental straight to production?"

"It'd be my pleasure." Dane grinned, and Camilla returned his sentiment.

"See ya around, Levi," he said, and with the girls' bags in one hand, he placed the other to the small of Camilla's back and ushered her outside.

Before Ivy could make her way out the door, I reached out and gently grabbed her wrist. She turned on her heel, and her eyes met mine.

"You okay?" I asked, and she shrugged.

"Of course I'm okay. Why wouldn't I be okay?" Her voice was all off. Stiff. Jolted. Too damn disconnected.

"Honestly, I don't know," I responded. "But you're definitely acting like you're pretty pissed about something."

"Are you saying I'm acting like a bitch?" she spat and snagged her wrist from my grip with a quick yank of her arm.

My brow furrowed of its own accord. "You said it, not me."

"Yeah, but you're obviously thinking it."

Well, fuck, now I was definitely thinking it.

I didn't respond, though, just stared into her hardened emerald gaze.

And she stared right back.

I searched her eyes. But she gave nothing in return. Not a single inkling of what she was really thinking or feeling.

"Are you mad about what happened last night?" I finally asked when the silence between us stretched too thin to not break it.

"Why would I be mad about that?" she questioned. "We fucked. Big deal."

We fucked. Big deal.

Ivy's words had the strength of a thousand men pummeling my chest.

"Wow. Yeah. Okay," I muttered more to myself than her.

One last look into the eyes of what felt like a stranger and I decided, instead of falling into our old routine of an all-out verbal war, I'd take the high road.

"See ya around, Ivy," I said and turned around, leaving her standing by herself in the foyer.

I had no idea why, within an eight-hour span of time, Ivy had gone from a woman lying in my bed, kissing me with everything she had, to someone who acted like I'd pissed in her fucking Cheerios.

I didn't know what was going on with Ivy.

But you could guarantee, I'd sure as fuck figure it out.

CHAPTER
TWENTY

Ivy

MY HEAD WAS ONE HUNDRED SHADES OF FUCKED-UP. AND when I closed my eyes to reel in my dark and twisty emotions, all I saw was black.

Inside the set of Walter Gaskins's home, the walls of this remake might as well have been closing in on me.

I'd left Levi's house over four hours ago, and still, I couldn't shake him from my thoughts.

We'd had sex.

We'd fucked.

Big deal, right?

It had been inevitable. I mean, the way the sexual tension had built up between us, we were bound to break and give in to it.

But you hadn't just fucked last night...

All of the commotion on set, Hugo talking to the camera crew, Boyce discussing scene positioning and dialogue cues with Sal Marcello, the man who played the Cold-Hearted Killer in the film, it all faded away at the thought.

Only the erratic beating of my heart and unsteady breaths of my lungs filled my ears as the realization of all of it soaked into my pores, my thoughts, my fucking heart.

Last night with Levi hadn't just been fucking.

It'd been something else. It'd been more.

He made love to you.

And right on cue, there was my inner dialogue. My goddamn subconscious telling me all the things I needed to hear but didn't want to hear.

Instantly, the world felt closer to my eyes, and the air around me turned soupy, making it harder to breathe. A glossy sheen obscured my vision, and my thoughts scattered like there was an actual electrical storm in my head, too many short-circuits to make any sense. All the while, the only thing that persisted, the only thing that kept repeating inside my mind was, *Levi didn't fuck you last night. He made love to you. And you made love to him right back.*

It was too much.

He was too much.

My feelings for him…*too fucking much.*

It was for all of those reasons, why the instant the sun had risen into the sky, I'd snuck out of his room like a coward. Too scared to face him. Too overwhelmed to confront what I felt for him.

A shaky breath bubbled up from my lungs, and I knew I needed to get it together.

I walked off the set for a brief moment and found emotional shelter off to the side of the crowd made up by the cast and crew. I leaned my back against the wall and just focused on the simplest of tasks.

Breathe. Just breathe. In and out, Ivy.

I placed a hand to my chest, and every muscle inside my body felt tight. Even my face felt tight, like smiling just wasn't an option today. The usual calm and focus I maintained while I was working had been replaced by a carousel of thoughts and questions and fears.

Despite everything I'd been through with Levi, despite the way he'd hurt me, I was still falling for him.

You've already fallen.

The way he'd made me feel last night, the emotions, the vulner-ability, the fucking intimacy of it all… It overwhelmed me.

I was scared.

Scared I felt too much. Cared too much. Loved him too much.

I feared I'd passed the point of no return with him, and that was the most terrifying part of it all.

Levi Fox hadn't proven to be someone who was delicate with my heart. Ever since I'd met him, he'd been a wildfire, and I feared that if I handed him my heart and he hurt me again, all I'd end up with was an empty chest and a world of fucking pain.

My eyes took on a sheen of moisture again as tension built be-hind them.

Fuck, I needed to shake this off. Now wasn't the time or place for an emotional meltdown.

I had work to do.

A pivotal fucking scene in this movie.

The one where Grace goes into Walter Gaskins's house with-out backup.

The one where she finds Bethany Johnson already dead.

The one based on the real-life scene that sealed her fate.

I pushed myself off the wall and paced the small hallway be-hind the set.

If my limbs were moving, the anxiety clawing at my throat was gone.

Well, at least, I could ignore it for a while.

Otherwise, if I was standing still, if I was letting my mind con-sume me, the anxiety, the fear, it was still there, coursing through my veins as if it hitched a ride on my blood cells.

"Ivy!" Boyce's voice boomed from the set, and I sprung into ac-tion, moving out of the hallway and toward where he stood inside Walter Gaskins's living room.

"Where the fuck were you?" he spat toward me as I stepped through the makeshift front door.

God, he could be such a bastard.

Some days, he treated me so fucking nice, almost too nice.

And others, he acted like I was the biggest thorn in his side.

I'd be glad when this movie was finished filming just for the fact that I wouldn't have to deal with Boyce Williams any longer. Hell, I'd already updated my agent Jason and manager Mariah that I didn't want to work with him again.

"Just grabbed a quick drink of water," I responded and forced an amiable smile to my lips.

But Boyce gave zero fucks about my excuse or the smile.

"Well, your water break is wasting everyone's fucking time," he muttered just quiet enough that his words reached my ears alone.

If only Hugo Roman could actually hear Boyce in action, I think he'd also think twice again about hiring him as a producer on future projects.

But Boyce had proven to be a wolf in sheep's clothing. Sly and malicious, lately, he always made sure his outbursts and shitty comments toward me were under everyone else's radar but mine.

"All right, quiet on set, everyone!" Hugo yelled from his director's chair just as Boyce walked off the set.

"You ready?" Sal asked me quietly, and I nodded.

He was a good man, a fantastic actor, and if anyone could bring Walter Gaskins's role to life, it was him.

It wasn't an easy role to play, a serial killer who preyed upon young women, but Sal Marcello had proven over his fifteen-year acting career that he was a master at his craft and could take on any role. Even the antagonist.

"What about you?" I asked him, and he offered a soft little smirk.

"I was born ready."

I grinned at that, but it was brief once the realization of the scene we were seconds away from delving into hit me straight in the chest.

I thought about Grace.

I thought about Levi finding her.

And I thought about the fact that while she was dying in his arms and Walter Gaskins had been served his fate, "Blue Bayou" played in the background.

Obviously, that was a part of the real-life story no one else knew, but it was a powerful and painful aspect.

I guessed I could've told Hugo. I could've revealed the secret details Levi had shared with me last night. It would've only added to the film, made it more raw, more fascinating, more everything. But it wouldn't have felt right.

Those were his details to tell, not mine.

With a deep inhale, I thought about my lines, and I pushed my mind to step into Grace Murphy's shoes. I glanced down at my Cold PD costume, my gaze taking in the nameplate with her name.

And just before Hugo called "Action!" I looked out toward the cast and crew and met the midnight-blue gaze of a man who played on my mind like it was his own personal concert venue.

Levi stood off to the side. His face was tight and jaw was firm. I'd had no idea he was here. Had no idea when he'd arrived, but I knew this scene in particular had to be the most painful one for him to watch.

A reenactment of the day he lost Grace.

I averted my eyes and stared down at the little taped X's positioned around the floor of the living room set.

One breath. Two breaths. I pushed my mind to another world. Another reality. Another person's life.

"Action!" Hugo called.

And just like that, I was Grace Murphy.

I'd just arrived at the residence that had received a disturbance call from a neighbor. When they'd phoned in the concern, they'd told the 9-1-1 operator they'd heard female screams coming from this house. And they'd said they'd not only heard them right before they'd called in, but they'd heard them the night before too.

This was the home of Walter Gaskins.

A man whose wife had died a few years prior.

A man who had no children or female relatives to speak of.

A man who lived alone.

"Dispatch, this is Murphy. I've arrived at 33 Mirror Lane. Send backup," I said into the radio at my chest.

I should've waited for backup. But I couldn't.

I needed to go inside.

"Cold PD!" I yelled with three harsh bangs to the door.

No answer.

I did that two more times, but when no response was received, I went in alone.

My gut clenched with impending doom, because I knew, I just knew Bethany was inside. And I prayed I wasn't too late.

Four hard kicks to the worn wood of the front door with my boot and I gained entry.

Three steps into the front door, my gun was in my hands, and I scanned the room.

No one.

Poised and ready, I walked through Gaskins's living room, past the kitchen and dining room, and when I reached the hallway that led to the bedrooms, I moved down it slowly, eyes searching, senses alert.

Once I stopped my boots in front of the back bedroom, the one at the very rear of the house, I found the door shut.

Fear clawed at my throat, but I swallowed it down and pushed the door open.

Gun poised, I peered inside, and then, everything turned to pain.

My world crumbled down around me.

Every fear, every worst-case scenario, came to fruition.

Bethany.

She lay on the bed. Her blue lips parted, her empty eyes partially open, and the cause of her death evident in the purpled bruises around the ashen skin of her dainty neck.

A strangled sob bubbled up from my lungs.

Frozen in shock and dismay for one second too long, I let my guard down.

My emotions had made me vulnerable.

And Walter Gaskins was there, behind me, ready to capitalize.

"Goodbye, Grace."

■

"Cut!" Hugo called on take seven. He stood up from his director's chair and offered a few celebratory claps toward the set. "Bravo, everyone!"

I lay in Johnny Atkins's arms, my head resting on his thigh, my body in a puddle of prop blood.

He grinned down at me as he helped lift me to my feet, but I couldn't muster the same expression.

We'd shot this painful scene one too many times, and my head had to go to a far-too-dark place in order to execute it.

I was drained, emotionally, physically, mentally.

The emotional roller coaster that was Grace's story had officially taken its toll.

"I think we can call it a day," Hugo added, and everyone on set offered a thankful cheer.

As I headed toward my trailer, an unwelcome voice filled my ears.

"Ivy!" Boyce called from behind me, and I grimaced. "Come here for a minute."

I paused my steps and turned to find him standing only a few feet in front of me.

With two long strides, he closed the distance between us, and I internally cringed at the close proximity to a man who'd proven time and time again he was fifty percent asshole and fifty percent egotistical bastard.

"You think you can come to work tomorrow a little more focused?" he questioned, and his harsh gaze locked with mine. "A scene that should've taken two takes max ended up being seven because of your inability to do what we needed you to do."

My brow furrowed at his unforgiving words. "I'm a little confused, Boyce," I responded. "Hugo seemed really happy with how filming went today."

"Happy with everyone else *but* you," he added, and even though his voice was quiet, his words boomed inside my head.

"And why isn't he telling me this himself?"

"Because he has better things to do than deal with the bullshit of a diva actress."

What a dick.

I'd thought I was on emotional overload a few minutes ago after finishing filming one of the hardest scenes of my acting career, but I was wrong.

Now, I was on real overload.

Stick a fucking fork in me, I was done with a capital D.

My gut instinct told me he was full of shit and nearly everything that came out of this man's mouth was lies. But the insecure part of me said other things that had me second-guessing every-fucking-thing.

And insecurity, once you let it seep into your thoughts, was a fucking parasite. It'd latch on and prey on every little uncertainty you had.

Instead of making a big scene, I took the high road. And, honestly, I just didn't have the strength to deal with him.

"See you tomorrow, Boyce," I said, turning to walk away, and I didn't look back.

Once I stepped inside my trailer, I shut the door and inhaled a long breath.

I just need some peace and quiet, I thought as I unbuckled the prop Cold PD belt and gun holster and removed it from my hips.

But that peace and quiet only lasted for so long.

Two soft knocks to my door and I cringed.

So much for peace and quiet.

I wasn't sure who I'd see on the other side of my trailer door, but I prayed it wasn't Boyce.

After a quick turn of the knob and a gentle jerk of my arm, the door opened with ease, and I wasn't the least bit prepared for the man who stood on the other side.

Levi.

Just the sight of his handsome face and my heart started to race. My lungs constricted. And a million tiny butterflies fluttered inside of my belly.

Today of all days, he was the one man I didn't know how to face.

I didn't know what to say.

I didn't know how to act.

And more than that, I didn't understand how I could've let myself feel so fucking much for him. The way I felt when I looked into the depths of his blue eyes terrified the ever-loving shit out of me.

CHAPTER
TWENTY-ONE

Levi

WHILE WATCHING IVY AND SAL AND JOHNNY FILM THAT FINAL scene, I had stood there and let all of the real-life memories flood my brain. They had effervesced to the surface and, for the first time in a really long time, I'd let myself really feel them.

God, today had been rough, a real fucking doozy of a day. And now, even though the sun was setting in the west, I stood in front of Ivy's trailer door, and I felt like the day was only just beginning.

Despite the risk of emotional overload, I wanted to see her. *Needed* to see her.

I needed to know why, after I'd made love to her—because that's what I'd done—how she could just write it off as a mere fuck, a simple, emotionless notch on a bedpost.

After two knocks to the door, Ivy opened it, and when her big green eyes met mine, I didn't miss the surprise that flashed within them.

But that surprise only lasted seconds.

Quickly, and without hesitation, she hid that surprise behind a mask of irritation.

"Got a minute to chat?" I asked, and she offered a small shrug of her petite shoulders.

"I guess so," she muttered and opened the door to her trailer wide enough to allow me to step in.

She shut the door behind us, and instead of meeting my gaze again, she walked over to the small vanity mirror and busied herself with a wet washcloth, scrubbing it harshly against the skin of her cheeks.

I didn't say anything to her at first, just watched as she removed the layers of makeup and fake blood from her skin.

"Is there something in particular you want to talk to me about? Or am I supposed to guess?" she questioned, transparent bubbles of anger forming from her words and popping right in front of my eyes.

She was pissed at me. I had no idea why. But Ivy's emotions were not easily hidden on her beautiful face. Her pain, her rage, it was evident in the crease of her lovely brow and the down-curve of her full lips.

But her eyes, they showed her soul, and when they locked with mine in the reflection in the mirror, I knew all the beauty of the universe could not even hope to compete with the passion and fire and incandescence those emerald orbs held.

And it was all of that passion and fire that put up the strongest fight.

"Did I miss something?" I questioned, and her gaze widened.

"Miss something?"

"Yeah," I responded, and I couldn't stop the grim chuckle that escaped my lips. "Did I miss something between last night and now?"

She set the washcloth down on the vanity, her skin now clear of makeup and reddened from her ministrations, and turned to meet my steady gaze.

"Obviously, you have a point to make here, but you'll have to

stop talking in fucking riddles for me to understand what you're trying to get at."

Her words struck a nerve.

Hell, they lit a match to that nerve and burst the damn thing
into flames.

"Fine," I said harshly. "Instead of nicely broaching this subject,
I'll play it your way. Why are you acting like such a cold-hearted
bitch to me?

"Excuse me?" she questioned, outrage spilling past her lips in a
rush.

"You heard me. Why are you acting like a cold-hearted bitch?"
I repeated my words. "Because, last night, when you were clawing
your fingers up my back and coming hard around my cock, you
seemed to enjoy my presence. But today, well, that appears to be a
different story. So, please, fucking enlighten me, sweetheart. Why
the sudden change?"

"You have a lot of fucking nerve!" she exclaimed, pointing a
shaking index finger directly at my face and moving toward me. But
her steps faltered when she closed the distance between us.

"I have a lot of nerve?" I asked on a bitter laugh. "Pretty sure I
wasn't the one begging to put my cock inside you last night. That
was all you, sweetheart."

"Yeah," she retorted. "But I'm pretty sure you didn't mind
sticking your dick inside me. Hell, you didn't mind so much that
you didn't even think twice about not using a condom and coming
inside of me bare."

Fuck. My eyes widened. Had I really not used a condom last
night?

It only took a few seconds of searching my memories to realize
her words were one hundred percent truth.

I'd lost myself in her so much that I hadn't even thought about
protection.

Hell, if anything, I subconsciously didn't want to use protection.

If it had been anyone else, it would've been my first thought.

But not with her. Not with Ivy.

With her, I turned into a fucking caveman who felt desperate about marking her. Claiming her. Making her mine.

"God, Ivy, I'm so sorry," I finally responded and meant every word.

"Do you fuck a lot without protection?" She put a defiant hand to her hip. "Because that'd be a good thing for me know."

"Fuck without protection?" I repeated her words. "First of all, sweetheart, you and I both know we didn't *fuck* last night. It was a hell of a lot more than that, even if you refuse to admit it to yourself. And secondly, no. I *always* use protection. But for some reason, when it comes to you, I do the complete fucking opposite of what I normally do."

"The complete fucking opposite of what you normally do?" she spat. "What is that supposed to mean?"

"Isn't it obvious?" I retorted. "You make me *fucking crazy*. You make me lose all sense of rational thought. Whether we're fighting or kissing or my cock is so deep inside you I don't know where I end or you begin, I lose my fucking mind when I'm with you."

The fight in her eyes left at my words, and I reached out and pressed my hand to the soft skin of her cheek. "I didn't fuck you last night, Ivy," I whispered.

A soft and shaky gasp left her lips, and she shut her eyes tightly. But it was too late, a small little tear slipped past her lids and started to make its descent down her cheek.

I caught it with my thumb, and for the briefest moment, her face curled up with emotion at the feel of my touch.

But then, like a damn wildfire had exploded inside of her veins, she abruptly pulled herself away from me. With both hands, she shoved into my chest in a weak attempt to put even more distance between us.

"This is too much!" she exclaimed, and her tear-stained gaze locked with mine. "Stop doing this to me!" she shouted, her voice growing more strained and pained with each word. "After everything that's happened, I don't think I can trust you, Levi. And I sure as hell don't want to feel this much for you."

Between Ivy's sudden frigidness toward me this morning, her anger and emotion now, and the fact that I'd just watched her act out *the* scene, I felt like I'd aged ten years.

A thousand pounds of stress and guilt and sadness and anxiety sat on top of my shoulders. Too many memories had bubbled up at the surface while watching Ivy portray Grace's death, how it all had really gone down, and for the first time since it had happened, I just didn't want to hold them inside anymore.

I didn't care about hiding them from everyone else, but I couldn't hide them from her anymore. I wanted her to know *everything.*

"*You* feel too much?" I questioned, and a million emotions flooded my veins. "How do you think I feel?" I said, and my words might as well have been a fucking lash, leaving my lips and snapping back with a bite.

I moved one step toward her, but she took two back.

"Do you understand how hard this has been for me, Ivy?" I continued, even though she was trying her damnedest to put space between us. She needed to hear these words, my words, my goddamn truth. "You are playing the part of the woman I loved! The woman I thought I would marry! The woman I lost!"

She gasped and put a shocked hand to her lips, but that didn't stop me, didn't stop the rush of words that flowed from my lips like water from a broken faucet.

"Grace was obsessed with finding the Cold-Hearted Killer. She was desperate to find Bethany, and that very desperation made her reckless."

I could see Grace's face in my mind the night I'd caught her in the station after hours looking through files. The dark circles under her eyes had turned into real bruises, and her skin had looked nearly translucent.

"So fucking reckless that I had to tell the chief to take her off the case. She was too goddamn connected, taking too many risks, putting herself out there every chance she got. She wasn't being safe or smart, and I loved her. I couldn't bear the thought of something happening to her. Which is really fucking ironic."

A harsh laugh escaped my lungs, and I paused with a grimace as a visual of Grace dead in my arms flickered behind my eyes.

Ivy stayed quiet, her lips still parted in shock, so I kept going.

"You can imagine that my role in taking her off the case didn't go well—that she didn't handle it well. She damn near had a mental breakdown, to be honest. And because of that, she ended up in Dr. Walter Gaskins's office."

Eyes wide, another gasp left her lips, but I couldn't stop now. I had to lay it all out.

"I was with her when he evaluated her. There to comfort her. Support her. Thought I was doing her a fucking favor since I'd been the one to push her to the brink."

I laughed, all bitter, no humor.

"She let me. We'd been fighting like cats and dogs up until that day, but finally, there in the office, she let go of it all and used me for comfort." I shrugged, my voice quiet. "It was obvious…that the two of us loved one another. And for Walter, that meant she went from a police officer he was treating for extreme anxiety and depression to his next victim."

I ran a hand through my hair and took a deep breath, preparing to unleash the final blow of Grace's and my truth.

"Walter Gaskins killed because he hated the idea of new love. In some weird, fucked-up way, I honestly think he thought he was doing the girls he killed a favor. Like saving them from feeling what he had to feel when his wife Betty died was a *good* thing," I said, my voice dropping to a near whisper. The truth was becoming more painful with each word. But I stayed strong. For Ivy. I pushed past the discomfort and told her the rest.

"After that moment in the office, he came up with a plan for Grace. Lured her to his house with a bogus disturbance call to her direct number. As if he was a trusted, frightened citizen of the town who needed help. She had a big heart and a soft spot. She called to tell me she was going, but she didn't wait for me to get there before going inside," I whispered.

"She wasn't a police officer who died in the line of fire," I admitted aloud for the first time ever. "She was a victim. Just like the rest."

I rubbed at the ache in my chest, and the pressure made my voice turn hoarse. "Because of me. Because she *loved me*. If we hadn't been in a relationship, she never would've been on Gaskins's radar. She would still be alive."

Ivy's mouth moved, open and closed as she tried to find words, but I didn't wait for them to form. I had to finish. I *needed* to be done.

"Besides Chief Pulse and me, no one else knows the real story. We swept all the painful details under the rug out of respect for Grace and her family."

"Why are you telling me this?" Her voice was quiet as a mouse, timid and careful and shaking. I locked my eyes with hers so hard that I gave her no room to break the connection.

"Because I had to tell you. I wanted to tell you. I fucking *needed* to tell you. Don't you see it, Ivy? You've stolen my fucking heart," I said, and that very heart responded by pounding hard and relentlessly against my ribs. "A heart that wasn't even supposed to beat anymore. One that didn't want to feel *any-fucking-thing*." My voice dropped lower, deeper, as each word that left my lips held every emotion rushing through my mind, my body, my fucking soul.

"But you've *wrecked me*," I said and inhaled a long breath as I found the strength to lay it all out there. "There is no going back for me, Ivy. Last night, at my house, that wasn't sex or fucking. That was me *making love to you*."

CHAPTER
TWENTY-TWO

Ivy

H E WAS QUIET, WAITING FOR ME TO RESPOND, AND THE SKIN OF his hands was mottled white with the pressure from the clench of his fists.

He'd been bottled, corked, and sealed from any and all emotion for so long, and now that he'd released the stopper, he was dangerously close to exploding.

I searched my manic mind, trying to settle on one single thought or feeling, but the effort was torture. All of it was at odds, too mashed up, and anytime I thought I might be latching on to how to feel, something else would come out of the back and smash it with a goddamn hammer.

And God, his vulnerability, it was there, so deeply evident within every facet of his expression, but it made me feel too many things. Hurt. Pain. Discomfort. *Relief.*

Finally, he was opening up to me.

Finally, he was letting me inside.

But I couldn't stop myself from being angry over the fact that he had been lying to me about so many things all along. It was like I'd been playing some sort of game with him, but only he had known the actual rules.

My heart raced and my thoughts turned to scattered chaos.

What were we even doing here? How was I supposed to make sense of anything that had ever happened between us? Even our softest moments, moments of commonality found in the desire to keep the movie true to the story, were shot to shit. The events were heartbreaking—*mutilating*—but they only made the disarray between us more of a mess.

"Everything," I whispered, the magnitude of the word making my voice shake. "*Every* painfully extracted thing between us has been a lie."

"Ivy, you know that's not true—"

My head shook, permission from my brain coming without premeditation as his words made me even angrier. "*Stop*. Don't fucking insult me. All I've known between us is anger and lust and a fucked-up mix of the two while you've been stewing on the answers the whole time. All you had to do was tell me. All you had to do was—"

"I'm doing it now," he interrupted, cutting into my ramble and the air with the same sharp blade. His voice was crisp and unyielding, as though I was supposed to just fall willingly at his feet.

"It's a little fucking late."

His mouth turned firm, and the line of his jaw straightened with impossible pressure. I couldn't understand how a person could grimace so hard without shattering their teeth, but Levi managed it. He managed that look all the fucking time.

"I didn't trust you," he pushed, taking two giant steps forward. My hands shook as I jumped back to avoid his advance and bumped into the small dressing table at the side of the room.

I laughed, a caustic, droning sound, as I swallowed the thick bile of irony. "Yeah, well, now *I* don't trust *you*."

All of the rigidity left his body like it'd been let out through a previously locked door. The tension in his face softened, his eyes lost the harsh glitter they so often carried, and just one gently curled hand smoothed softly down the line of my jaw.

It was intimate—startling.

It was all the physical touch I needed to remind me of our night together.

"I know you don't. But I do. God, Ivy, I trust you more than I've ever trusted anyone. More than—"

Stubborn tears pooled at the corners of my eyes before spilling over the dam and paving tracks down my cheeks. I shook my head, fighting the touch of his hand and the soothing affection in his voice. I didn't want to be affected. I didn't want to give him any of myself. I didn't want his soft words or honest confessions, and most of all, I didn't want the hope that there was a real possibility Levi and I could be together, that we could be *something*.

Good God, I didn't want to fucking hope.

"Stop," I ordered, the word catching on what would have been a sob if I'd let it. Instead, I choked it, guarding it with steel and whatever remnants were left of my battered heart.

I wouldn't be swallowed up by Levi Fox. Not now, not one day, not fucking ever.

Right?

His words were whispers, but what they lacked in volume, they made up for in everything else. They were honest and considerate, and they were wholly flattering. "I know you don't trust me. And I don't expect you to. But you're everything I never knew I wanted and then some. You're the perfect mix of backbone and nurture and just stubborn enough to put up with me. You've got a brilliant mind and a load of talent, but you still care about what matters. You use your head when you want to use your heart, and fuck, Ivy…you did everything you could to look out for a man who sure as fuck didn't look out for you."

My cheeks pinked and my stomach flipped, unable to resist the warming glow of compliments as powerful as the ones he'd just given. He, Levi Fox—the most callous, broody guy I'd ever met—was waxing poetic…about me.

"You don't have to trust me yet because I'll wait. I'll wait for you to understand how much I trust you, and I'll wait for you to feel like I've earned yours. Ivy, I promise…I'll wait."

With one soft sweep of my jaw and a kiss to the apple of my cheek, Levi turned and left me.

Left me to his words and my thoughts and the swirl of everything he'd told me about his and Grace's truth.

Left me to decide.

■

Levi's clothes effectively removed from my dresser, I slammed the drawer shut.

I'd meant to launder and return them quickly after changing out of them at his house the night after the hospital.

But the twisted part of me had packed them up in my bag and taken them to our new rental property. The place was way less exciting than Grace's old house, with white walls and store-bought furniture. The styling was modern rather than quaint farm, and I missed the comfort her house provided when I was feeling too raw.

I knew staying there should have had the opposite effect, but her walls were friendly. She was welcoming in a way I hadn't expected when I'd first accepted the role, and her little house always seemed to be good for advice on how to handle things I was otherwise wholly unfamiliar with.

I wasn't Montana born and raised, and I didn't have the experience with small-town residents. But around every corner, there was a clue. Whether it was her grandfather reaching out to share some wisdom or a thoughtfully placed snow scraper on the front porch,

Grace had prepared me for all the things I hadn't thought about facing.

But now, I was on my own, forced to come to some hard decisions without her guidance.

Given Levi's revelations about the nature of their relationship, and my very complicated feelings for him, maybe the departure of her spiritual guidance was for the best.

"Hey, Ivy Belle," Camilla muttered, just her head poking through the small gap she'd created between the door and the frame. "Is it safe for me to come in?"

My brow furrowed, and my attitude peaked. "Why the hell wouldn't it be safe?"

Her smile was indulgent. "Oh, I don't know. Maybe because you've been slamming shit around in here for the last five minutes loudly enough that I could hear you from down the hall."

The wrinkle between my brows reformed at the sides of my mouth as I scowled. "I wasn't banging stuff around."

She scooted through the door and sashayed to my bed, settling herself on top of one pretzeled leg and wrapping the arms of her sweatshirt tighter around her chest. "Uh, yeah. You were."

I stuck out my tongue and sighed. "Stop being such a know-it-all."

She shrugged with a laugh and snuggled deeper into the cotton of her sweatshirt. "I can't help it if I know everything."

The statement itself was innocent in all of its properties, but the weight it settled on my shoulders wasn't by coincidence.

Because Camilla didn't know everything. She might know me well and her intuition was spot-on, but Levi hadn't spilled all the private details of the real Cold-Hearted Killer story to her that afternoon.

No. He'd shared it all with *me*.

Grace's obsession, their relationship, her discovery about the killer, and what it'd meant for the two of them. His *guilt* over all of it.

It was perhaps the only thing he hadn't actually admitted—how culpable he felt over his role in her death. But he hadn't needed to mention it. It'd clung to the walls and coated my skin, and now, hours later, I was still covered in the vile emotional punishment he'd assigned himself as a result.

Camilla's voice was soft, but it still startled. "Hey," she called, only a foot from my face. When my eyes met hers, her body language turned nurturing. "God, you look exhausted," she cooed, moving with me until I settled onto the bed. "Get some rest, okay? I talked to Mary earlier and Sam is doing just fine. Giving them hell already apparently. But if that's what's got you so twisted, you don't need to worry."

I nodded and lay back on the bed until my head dented the soft pillow, letting her believe Sam's well-being was the main catalyst for my anguish. It wasn't that sharing with my sister was something I wanted to avoid; I just didn't have the energy. Cam sat there and stroked my hair until, eventually, I settled.

Settled into a restless night and tortured dreams of a man I couldn't forget—only now, I wasn't sure I wanted to.

CHAPTER
TWENTY-THREE

Levi

GASPED AS I WOKE ABRUPTLY FROM A SOUND SLEEP. I WASN'T SURE what had woken me, but I was sure, despite the unexpected wake-up, I hadn't felt this rested in years.

Light from the clock glared in the still blackness of my quiet bedroom, and I craned my neck to get a better look at the time. Just past two a.m., it was hardly what any sane human would consider morning.

I rolled over and snuggled deeper into my pillow, intent to find the comfort of sound sleep again. Tangible and close, it seemed achievable.

Apparently, getting everything off of my chest that afternoon had gone a long way in making some of my unrest disappear. I felt ready to let the past go. Ready to embrace the present.

Ready to dream of a future.

I sighed and closed my eyes.

But the sound of tinkling bells and an organ bass startled them open again. Obnoxious and overzealous, the doorbell was the exact one my mother had had installed in my much smaller childhood home the year before she left.

If anyone had used it in the years I'd lived here since, I might have actually remembered to change it. As it was, a wave of nostalgia and a renewed sense of agitation washed over me.

I shook my head to myself. Self-actualized serenity never lasted long in the world of Levi Fox.

With a grunt and a curl, I pulled my body up and out of the bed with the muscles of my core. I wasn't dressed to impress in a pair of black boxer briefs and nothing else, but whoever dared ring my doorbell at two in the morning would have to be ready to face the consequences.

The hall was quiet and dark as I trudged down it, but the air felt tangible. It poked and prodded at me, urging me to wake up fully and come out of the haze of sleep.

Immediately alert at the unwelcome unease, I moved quickly down the stairs and opened the door without preamble. I'd been trained in stealth and caution as an officer of the law, but I'd also been trained in common sense. Regardless of any foreboding dread, I doubted seriously that someone with the intent to harm me would have bothered to ring the bell.

Ivy was halfway down the steps on the way back to her car.

"Ivy," I called out to make her stop.

Her steps halted, but she made no move to turn. The back of her sweater bunched, and her shoulders rose to meet her ears.

"Ivy," I called again. "Turn around."

The unapologetic order got her attention. Winged and free, her mane of fiery hair swung out in a crescent as she spun to face me. I settled into the doorframe, crossing my feet at the ankles and my arms over my chest. The casual nature of my stance only geared her up more.

"I don't know why I came here."

I shrugged. "I don't either."

Her eyes narrowed and her anger grew, and I had to work not to smile. I hadn't realized it quickly enough, but I *loved* to watch her hackles rise.

"Jesus!" she shouted. "I don't know what I was thinking." She turned back down the steps and headed for her car again, but I didn't move from my spot. I watched the way she moved—attitude bleeding from even the simplest of actions—and waited for my moment.

Her hand clasped on the handle of her car door, and I smiled as she paused. She wanted to be here. She wanted the fight. She wanted a me-and-her, and she wanted it in a way that burned her badly enough to come here in the middle of the night.

"You were thinking about me," I challenged.

Her hair flicked again, another dramatic turn toward me in the books, and the emerald of her eyes shone in the moonlight. "Excuse me?"

"I said, *you were thinking about me.* That's what brought you here in the middle of the night, and that's what'll keep you coming back forever."

She abandoned the car then, charging me so fiercely she barely pulled her body to a stop before colliding with me.

"You are *such* an egotistical prick!"

"Yeah, baby," I agreed with a taunting smile. "I am."

"Argh!" she screamed into the quiet, cold night. Her breath formed a cloud of lust between us, and I had to work to keep myself from wrapping my arms around her and pulling her into the house by force. "I can't believe I'm here again! I can't believe we're *fighting!*"

"Believe it, baby. You're here because you're meant to be."

"Oh, right. I'm meant to be," she retorted sarcastically. I itched to put my hands on her, but I knew if this was going to stick, if we'd ever make it all the way past this push and pull, she was going to have to be the one to give in. She had to be the one to *need* me. I already knew I needed her. "And the fighting?"

"Don't you know by now?" I asked softly, the roughness in my still sleepy voice devolving to full gravel. "Fighting, for us, means *feeling*. And there weren't ever two people who've felt more for one another than you and I do."

Her lips, her eyes, the soft curve of her cheek, I ran my eyes over it all, memorizing a course for when I finally got to use my lips. She was still anxious, bouncing all over the place as she tried to work through the fear of giving in.

"What? So we're just meant to fight for the rest of our lives? That's ridiculous!"

My smile was bold and unrepentant at the mention of *the rest of our lives*.

"It's not," I challenged, finally straightening to my full height. "It's us and it's real."

"And how the fuck is that supposed to be sustainable, Levi?"

"Because as much as I fight you, I'd fight a million times harder *for* you."

She was breathing hard and her eyes were wet, and my heart felt like it would explode in my chest.

"Sweat and blood, life and death, I'd give it all for you. Anytime. Anywhere. You're worth it. You're...*worth* it."

Her body hit mine hard. Violent and unchecked, she gave herself over to me and us and everything the moment meant.

It was her and me, and we were *something*.

It defied nature and sensibility, but it was authentic. It was right. And she and I would be a story people talked about for the rest of their lives.

Angry, urgent lips covered mine and grappled for control. I gave it over to them immediately, knowing I didn't need to lead this dance to enjoy it. Sometimes the manliest thing a guy could do was surrender himself to the wants and directions of a woman.

It was trust embodied, and just like the chief had taught me, actions almost always spoke louder than any and all words.

I pulled her back into the house and slammed the door, backing us up to the stairs and bringing her down on top of me.

She licked and sucked at my throat, and I groaned as she touched the sensitive spot behind my ear.

"Ivy," I whispered, the two-syllable name sounding grittier than it ever had.

I settled my hips into one of the steps and put my back to the riser, and my little redhead didn't waste the opportunity. She climbed astride me and pressed her knees into the carpet runner, fusing her hips to mine and grinding.

My back lodged into the riser, and suddenly, I decided taking some of the control wouldn't be so bad.

In one swift move, I stood, wrapping my hands around her ass and lifting her with me. She gasped, and I used the opening to push my tongue deeper into her mouth. Her tongue was creamy and rich, and her breasts pushed tight against my chest on reflex.

I was feeling entirely similar, unable to get close enough, fighting the need to drop her right there on the stairs again and shove myself inside.

I wanted to take my time, work her body inch by inch until I covered them all and looped back again.

Hard and fast would be good sometime, but now, I wanted to *savor.*

Her skin. Her lips. Her pussy.

Taste and smell and touch, I planned to entwine myself in each and every one of them until she couldn't remember a time when she wanted to be anywhere but under me.

I turned and jogged up the stairs, taking my lips off of hers for just long enough to make it to the top. She kept hers active, though, smoothing them over the skin of my neck and moving them down to the bare top of my collarbone.

Hard and ready, my cock pushed against her thin pajama pants and fought with the two measly layers of fabric between it and sweet solace.

I'd been inside her before, and I remembered how powerful the connection had felt.

Now I just had to see if she did.

CHAPTER
TWENTY-FOUR

Ivy

LEVI'S STEPS WERE HURRIED AS HE MOVED US UP THE STAIRS AND down the hall to his bedroom. I'd been there before—could tangibly picture the memory—but the whole place felt new.

But it wasn't the old house with its high ceilings and ornate fixtures changing the feel, it was the synchronization of us.

For so long, so many weeks and weeks, we'd been fighting this—fighting the possibility of one another. Even when we came together, the terms were rigid and the connection superficial.

Bodies, pleasure, and a means to a tension-filled end, we'd needed each of those releases.

But now, I needed *him*.

His body was better than I'd ever imagined it could be, and I ached with the demand to have him inside.

Moving and stroking, I wanted to feel his skin on the most sensitive part of mine.

"Levi," I urged.

He nodded as he settled me on the bed and came down on top. Our bodies never broke, but the delicious feel of his weight made it feel like we'd been separated by miles before.

"Please," I begged, and I felt the line of his mouth curve against my neck. He groaned there, coating me with the vibration and making my legs tighten further around his hips. "I need you inside of me."

His head shook slightly, his lips skating along my skin on their journey to my mouth. His eyes were alight, and his hair was fully mussed as he smiled against the flesh of my lips and finished it with a nip.

"You don't have to beg, Ivy. You couldn't bribe me to delay this."

A tingle tickled the line of my spine and buzzed through my head. I felt overwhelmed—almost drugged—by the intoxicating hum of avid participation.

We both wanted this—wanted each other—without a hint of regret.

Fingers bent, he dragged his hands up under my sweatshirt without stopping at the top, so I lifted my hands to ease his endeavor.

My bare skin pebbled in the dry, heated air, and my nipples stood up to peaks immediately.

He was ravenous, nearly insatiable, as he feasted on the newly uncovered bounty. The flesh of my breasts malleable and thick, he bunched them in his palms and sucked one nipple and then the other into his mouth.

I slid my hands down his back, scratching at the smooth, tanned skin with my nails until I made it to the waistband of his boxer briefs. I pushed and tugged, trying to force them over the cheeks of his ass, and he lifted his hips in an attempt to help me.

But his cock was too big and too long, and the front of his boxers wasn't so willing to cooperate.

He stood up without prompting and pushed them down to the floor, and I got to watch.

Thick and sinewy, his muscles were defined under the surge of adrenaline. His veins stood out in relief, and I had to bite the flesh of my bottom lip to stop myself from coming.

Restless, I rocked on the bed, reaching up with my hands to call all of that perfect naked body back to me.

His smirk was devilish as he shook his head. "Not yet, baby. Your turn."

I started to push at my pants and panties, but he didn't make me do the work for long. He took over with ease and practice, ridding me of the pants and underwear in one smooth swoop.

"God, Ivy," he groaned. "You are *perfect*."

His weight came back quickly, and he scooted me up the bed. I went willingly with his every direction, raising my arms above my head to give him better access to full-body contact.

Instead, he paused at the movement of my hands and watched, reaching up with one of his own to pull them back.

Wrinkles pulled at the skin between my eyes as I tried to understand, but the mystery didn't last long. He brought both hands to the space between us and studied them. The fingers, the palms. The scar from the coffee burn that first day at the station.

Tender and swift, he pressed his lips to the injured skin and breathed through his nose. Regret clouded the air between us, a physical, rolling cloud as it drifted off him.

"I'm sorry," he said, his voice no more than a breath.

The very last of the tension melted from my shoulders and into the bed, clearing the space between us for good.

Loving me slowly, he kissed my arms, my body, and freed my mind when he finally slid slowly inside—and turned everything I knew about sex, love, and affection upside down.

■

How could a man who was so rough in conversation be so soft in bed?

It was an unending question—for I feared I'd never have the answer.

After our first time having sex, I'd assumed the gentleness with which he'd treated me was a fluke. But two times down—two times he'd done his best to handle me with a careful firmness—I was beginning to think it might be more than that.

I stroked the skin of his chest, counting his steady, even breaths on the end of every exhale. He was up to 1,547 by the time I realized he hadn't been sleeping, as previously suspected, for any of it.

"What's on your mind?" he whispered into the top of my hair.

"Dichotomies."

His chest jerked under my cheek, and a small air-filled chuckle rolled gently into the silence. "Shit, Ivy."

The teasing tone of his condescension brought my head up and around, but I kept my body lax. Evidently, orgasms were a good mood stabilizer. "What?"

"Only you could be thinking about something as complicated as dichotomies during the post-coital glow."

"Hey, it's your fault," I defended. "You're the one who holds conversations like every word is part of a full-frontal attack and then makes love like he's disarming a bomb. *You're* the contradiction."

"Makes love?" he asked softly, one gentle hand tangling easily into the tresses of my hair and then smoothing through to the ends.

I settled my chin on a hand on his chest. "I seem to remember you not liking when I called it fucking."

He smiled, big and open, and the corners of his mouth made it all the way to his beautiful blue eyes. They were clearer like this—almost crystalline in nature—and he finally seemed to be at rest from the inside out. "Yeah," he agreed. "Fucking is great. I've used it as an outlet for stress more times than you want to know."

I scowled, and unbelievably, his grin only grew.

"But not me and you," he whispered. "No matter how rough,

how raw, how energized—no matter what we try—fucking will never be a good name for what we do."

My skin tingled at the suggestion of all the ways we could be intimate with one another and the obvious promise that he would see to our accomplishment of all of them.

It made me think about everything he'd been through, everything he'd seen and lived in his life.

Everything he'd told me so confidentially.

"I won't ever tell anyone," I said softly.

His head jerked, and the space between his eyes narrowed as he searched mine. He was trying to follow how I'd gotten there—what I meant—but the chances he would get there without some explanation were pretty slim.

I was aware of the mental jump I'd made, even if I wasn't completely sure how it'd come about.

"About everything you told me. You and Grace and what really happened," I expanded. "I understand why you kept it a secret. I understand, and I respect it. I won't tell anyone with production or anyone outside of it. I won't tell *anyone*."

His mouth moved from a curve to a line, and I had a twinge of regret for ruining his good mood. But it was important that he knew—important enough to ruin the moment if necessary.

"I'm sorry to bring it up." He sighed, but I pushed forward. "But I'm more sorry I threw it in your face earlier."

The brittle shell he'd pulled into place cracked a little as he tucked some of my hair behind my ear. "It's not that, Ivy. I don't blame you for being upset before, and I can't tell you how much it means to me that you're willing to keep all of this to yourself."

My eyebrows drew together as I tried to figure out what that left to be upset about. "Okay...then why did your face turn—"

"Into an asshole again?" he interjected, and I laughed a little.

"Well...yeah."

His sigh was heavy, but he tempered the impact by wrapping his arms around my back and running a finger through my hair.

"Because I have more to tell you. The rest of the story."

"The rest?"

He nodded and searched my eyes. I thought at first it might be to see how I was feeling, but after a few moments, the real purpose became clear.

He was looking for a life raft.

Unease and unrest swirling in his gut, he was worried about telling me whatever was left.

"Go ahead," I urged, despite the newfound pit in the bottom of my stomach. What the hell else was he hiding?

"Grace was pregnant."

I gasped, the fingers of one hand shooting up to cover my mouth. He closed his eyes tightly at the sound, and I watched, transfixed, as a single plump tear rolled gently down from the outside corner of his eye.

With a gentle sweep, I wiped the tear away, hoping it was linked to his pain.

"Levi," I breathed.

"It was really early. Six weeks. She hadn't told me, and I don't even think she knew. But the autopsy…" He choked, and I forced a sob back down my throat.

"Oh, Levi," I soothed, pressing my lips to his cheek and watching, stunned, as two of our tears mingled on his face.

"Red covered it up. Asked the new coroner not to put it in the report. They'd been friends since they were kids, so he did it. No one knows except the two of us." He grinned, though there was no happiness in it. "Well, the three of us now."

"Why? Why hide it?"

"It felt wrong, adding to everyone's burden. It felt wrong telling everyone when Grace didn't even know. And it felt wrong, giving

Gaskins another victim."

My heart trilled and spasmed as I worked to make room in my heart. By giving myself over to Levi, I was giving myself over to a hell of a lot more. Grace, and everything she stood for. Levi's pain at the loss of her and the effects of a relationship unresolved. And a tiny beginning of a baby, one who never got the chance to be loved.

Levi would walk through fire for the people he cared about; or in this case, he'd lovingly carry the entire load. Grace's family didn't have to hurt because Levi took on the pain for them.

"You're a hero hidden in an asshole, Levi Fox."

He smiled then. Even laughed—a small rolling chuckle.

"You're an angel hidden in…" I raised a brow, challenging him to finish the rest. But he was ready for the test, and he'd studied all the right answers.

His wink was subtle but life-changing. "Hollywood. An angel hidden in Hollywood."

"Appropriate," I praised. "Los Angeles *is* the City of Angels."

■

"You sure you can't stay for some breakfast?" he asked as he pressed me into the hard metal of my car. Hands to my hips and eyes full of affection, he looked at me now in a way I'd only dreamed of in the past.

The morning air was soft and dewy with condensation and felt thick in my throat as I answered. "I wish I could, but I left without saying anything to Cam. I have to get back before she wakes up, and so I can get ready for work."

"I can't believe this is the last day of filming." His hands tightened to the point of almost pain on my hips. "I can't believe you'll be leaving soon." He laughed—just a tiny, broken chuckle. "I guess I'm finally getting what I wished for, huh?"

"We'll work something out."

The words were out before I even had time to consider them. Time to consider how ready I was to work to make them happen.

How to make them happen.

Levi had been right when he'd said fighting was part of feeling for us. But how could we focus on fighting each other when we had to fight the distance?

Levi leaned in and touched his lips to mine. His movements soft and slow, he swirled my tongue with his own and inhaled. In perfect unison, we stepped into bliss together and fell into an abyss.

I'd foolishly thought some of the appeal of Levi's kiss had been the unexpected. We'd almost always gone at one another without prior consent or intent, and the passion was the potion.

But I was wrong. It was just as good as all of the times we'd taken each other by surprise.

And this time, instead of an end to an argument, it was the beginning of something better.

CHAPTER
TWENTY-FIVE

Levi

THE WALL AT MY BACK WAS FIRM AND STEADY AS I LEANED AGAINST it outside of Ivy's dressing room. She'd arrived over an hour ago and gone straight to makeup thanks to the long shooting schedule for the day, and I'd done my best to give her space.

I wasn't sure what she wanted the production team to know, and I certainly wasn't prone to letting strangers in on my business, so going full-on PDA as soon as she arrived didn't seem like an option.

But I was eager to feel her body in my arms, and I had been since the moment she'd pulled away that morning.

I nodded in hello as techies and lighting gurus and various behind-the-scenes people fluttered up and down the halls and tried to look as disinterested as possible.

My phone vibrated in my pocket as if it knew I needed a distraction.

My best friend Jeremy's name showed as the caller, so I swiped my finger across the screen and put it to my ear.

"Hey, Jer."

"Wow. So, you are still alive," he said by way of greeting. "I honestly wasn't sure anymore."

I rolled my eyes and pushed off the wall with my booted foot, walking up the length of it as I talked. I wasn't sure what it was about having a phone conversation, but I'd never been able to do it while standing still.

"Cute," I remarked.

"I'm always cute. You just haven't spoken to me in so long you've forgotten."

I chuckled a little, glancing up the hall when the commotion changed cadence. One after the other, Ivy and Camilla power-walked into her dressing room and left the door open.

"Is someone maybe missing me a little bit?" I teased Jeremy as I walked casually back down the hall toward Ivy's door.

"You?" Jeremy scoffed. "Not many people miss assholes."

His insult was hollow no matter how cutting it seemed, and I didn't get offended by name-calling all that easily. If I did, I probably wouldn't be starting a relationship with the woman who'd christened me with more than her fair share of ugly monikers.

"I'll have you know one person likes me a lot."

Jeremy was quiet, serious. "The actress?"

I rolled my eyes and laughed. "Yeah, Jer. And she has a name."

"Wow. All that hating her is making a little more sense. Ironic, though, given, you know, your mom."

I shook my head and growled a little. "Yeah. Thanks for bringing that up."

"Better to face those demons now, dude," Jeremy advised. "The more you sweep under the rug, the more comes back to haunt you later on."

"Thank you for your sage wisdom," I murmured, stopping in front of Ivy's open door and finally catching her eye. "But I'm in control of this. One thing at a time."

She had on a plum-colored tank under a leather jacket, and all of her wild hair was smoothed to pin straight. Her green eyes glowed and her makeup was soft, but underneath all of the work they'd done to make her look like Grace, I could still see Ivy.

The curve of her hips, the swell of her chest. The set of her stance and the fire in her eyes. Those were all things even the best makeup crew in the world would have trouble hiding.

"Sure, sure," Jeremy mumbled. "You're in control."

"Listen, smartass. I'll call you soon. Set up something for the four of us, maybe."

"The four of us. Christ. Liza is going to lose her shit over this."

I glanced down the hall and then looked to the ground as I told him quietly, "Keep it to yourself, though. I don't know how many people we're ready to tell about being together."

Someone bumped me from behind, hard, and I startled. I spun with my hand to my gun at my hip, but I relaxed when I realized it was just Boyce not watching where he was going.

He didn't apologize for bowling into me, but that behavior was hardly anything new.

"I gotta go, Jer," I said, pulling the phone away from my ear and hanging up while he was still talking.

Fuck only knew what other kind of hell he planned on giving me, but I didn't like the idea of not keeping an eye out anytime Boyce and Ivy had a conversation.

I knew she wasn't comfortable around him. I mean, it didn't take much for anyone to see the physical evidence of her discomfort when Boyce was inside her personal space. It was visible in her tense shoulders, her firm mouth, and the way she wasn't as willing to freely share her thoughts or opinions when he was around.

Cam bustled around the room, shooting from one task to the next as Ivy stood by the dressing table in the corner and nodded along to Boyce.

"First up is the scene where Grace and Levi fight," Boyce began.

Ivy's brows drew together. "I thought that was one of the last scenes."

Boyce's posture turned edgy, and I took a step inside the room. Cam noticed and narrowed her eyes at the look on my face.

"Well, now, it's one of the first scenes," Boyce clipped. "It's happening today no matter what, so you should still be prepared, right?"

Ivy glanced to me, and erotic visions of her underneath me in the early hours of this morning flashed before my eyes. Her cheeks pinked and her voice deepened, and I knew she was thinking of the same thing.

"Of course, I'm ready."

Boyce scowled and dropped the rest of the schedule in her lap before storming out of the room and bumping me in the shoulder again as he did.

I didn't know what his fucking problem was, but I did know he didn't want to keep body checking me for much longer if he didn't want a consequence.

I moved deeper into the room, shutting the door behind me and closing myself in with the pair of sisters. Instantly, my gaze searched out Ivy, and I smiled when her emerald green eyes met mine.

Cam's voice dropped an octave and lilted with accusation.

"I *knew* there was something different about you today," she declared, pointing a finger in Ivy's direction. "What's going on with you two?"

Ivy smiled, and my whole world exploded. Happy thoughts and simple affection, she was *excited* when she thought about the two of us together.

Unwilling to let her color it as anything other than what it was, out of fear or uncertainty or deference to me, I slid an arm around her shoulders, pulled her close, and faced Camilla head on, declaring, "We're together."

"Together?" Cam asked. "Together as in…"

"Together," I repeated with a smile. "As in dating exclusively and planning to continue. As in, that thing we talked about over pastries a while ago is happening."

Ivy pulled at my arm, turning underneath it and narrowing her eyes. "What thing did you talk about?"

Camilla laughed. "He's talking about the fact that he intends to be my brother-in-law."

"What?" Ivy yelled, and I had to bite my lip to contain my roar.

"Not tomorrow, baby. Relax."

"You relax!" she shot back, and both Camilla and I lost the battle with restraining our laughter.

Ivy's face reddened slightly as she swung an angry hand between us. "So, what? The two of you are just going to gang up on me now?"

I leaned down and touched my lips to hers, and the rest of everything melted away. Ivy's pseudo-anger. Camilla's presence. The obstacles ahead of us.

All of it—gone.

Pliant and sure, her mouth molded itself to mine and moved in tandem. Her tongue was moist and soft, and the tip of it in my mouth felt like heaven.

"Oh God," Camilla finally groaned, but her voice was equal parts amusement and teasing.

I pulled away slowly, savoring the taste of Ivy's lips on my own. I wasn't even a little chagrined.

"Great," Cam muttered, but her lips crested up into a smile. "Well, ya little kissing bandit, you've got to be on set in two minutes, and your lipstick is ruined."

"Shit!" Ivy yelped, jumping up from her seat and rushing over to the mirror.

I moved to the dressing table and took a tissue to clean up the evidence I was certain coated my face. The reflection of the man staring back at me was impressive. He'd walked through hell, but somehow, someway, he'd come out the other side smiling.

COLD

■

Flowers and knickknacks littered Ivy's dressing room as I cruised the perimeter while I waited for her to get changed. It'd been a long day, but filming had finally wrapped. The crew would be here for a couple more weeks getting all sorts of B-roll and various town shots, but the moments in which Ivy Stone had to be Grace Murphy were over.

The knot in my chest unlooped as I pictured us being able to move on—as I pictured me being able to move on. It'd taken a full six years, but it was time, and Ivy and the movie were the catalysts.

I guess Old Red knew what he was doing, after all.

I smirked, thinking about my boss, a man who'd been my champion since before I'd known I needed one. He'd been a straight talker and a friend, but most of all, he'd been a guide even when I was reckless.

Ivy's voice carried down the hall, and my eyebrows drew together at how agitated she sounded.

I listened harder, staring at the dressing table as though it could help amplify the other sense, and then noticed what looked like a framed, candid picture of Ivy. The edges of the frame were ivory and stone, and I was almost certain I hadn't noticed it before.

I swiped it off the table and into my hand just as Ivy entered the room, an agitated Boyce hot on her heels.

"I'm not doing it, Boyce," Ivy declared, yanking at the sleeves of her leather jacket and pulling it off with a tug. "I'm sorry, but Hugo is happy with my performance, and so am I. I don't know why you're not on board, but you're going to have to get over it."

"Get over it?" he questioned scathingly. "I got you this job!" he yelled, moving quickly and getting right in her face, grabbing her violently by the upper arms. She flinched, and I relocated, immediately putting my body between hers and his and pushing him back two steps.

"Back off," I warned Boyce, a hand to his chest and fire in my veins. My heart was beating at triple its normal speed, and my focus was hypersensitive. The pulse in my head was intense as I tried to get control of my anger.

Goddamn, I wanted to knock his fucking lights out.

"You ever put your hands on her like that again, and I'll kill you myself."

His eyes were beady and defiant, and he foolishly showed no signs of heeding my warning. "Stay out of this," he ordered. "This film and how I handle my staff are none of your business."

With gritted teeth, I pulled my badge from my pocket and slipped it on my belt, making sure to tap it with a finger for extra effect. "That's where you're wrong. I'm a cop, I'm the official liaison to this movie for the department, and I'm Ivy's boyfriend. So, if you've got a problem with her, you've definitely got a problem with me."

Boyce snapped. "This guy?" he yelled, meeting Ivy's eyes around my shoulder. "A fucking small-town hick? Good going, honey. You can kiss your career goodbye."

"That's enough!" I yelled, using an easy hand to scoot him out the door. I didn't shove and I didn't hit, but the pressure in my hand was way more than a suggestion.

I was breathing heavily as Boyce stalked off down the hall, pushing PAs and various workers out of his way as he did.

It wasn't until I got back into Ivy's dressing room and closed the door behind me that I realized I still had that fucking frame in my hand.

Turning it horizontally, I held it up for Ivy to see. "You recognize this?"

She was quiet, reflective, even, as she studied the anger on my face, but she shook her head no.

And immediately, my stomach roiled.

Ripping off the back without finesse, I tossed it to the side and pulled out the photo. It was creepy in the way any truly candid photo was, and it'd obviously been printed on consumer paper rather than at a professional shop.

And inscribed on the back were two gut-churning words.

Love, Me.

"Fuck," I breathed, fighting the instinct to crumple the thing. I wanted to shred it, tear it into goddamn pieces, but I knew that wouldn't help a fucking thing when it came to evidence.

"That's it," I declared. "I'm done fucking around. I'm done living this sick shit, and I'm done thinking this is just some jokester. You're glued to my side, you hear me?" I ordered, pointing at Ivy.

She was shaking as Cam came through the door and jolted to a stop at the state of the two of us.

"Jesus," she murmured. "What's going on?"

I pulled my phone from my pocket and scrolled straight to the number for the chief as Ivy filled her in.

I didn't have the patience. I didn't have the time.

And I sure as fuck didn't have the stomach.

Goddamn, was this really my life *again*?

CHAPTER
TWENTY-SIX

Ivy

"**A**RE YOU SURE YOU DON'T WANT TO EAT SOMETHING?" Camilla asked over her shoulder as she loaded a few plates and utensils into the dishwasher.

"No," I responded from the couch. "I'm good, thanks."

"Have you eaten anything today, baby?" Levi asked beside me, and he pulled me closer into his side, gently tucking the afghan I was wrapped up in around my legs.

I shrugged. "I'm sure I ate something."

"No, you haven't," Camilla kindly offered from the kitchen. "You skipped breakfast, you were too busy to eat lunch, and you didn't eat a single bite of the pizza we had for dinner."

Normally, I was a scheduled eater. Three meals a day peppered in with some snacks, and I stuck to that regimen. Missing meals only happened when I was either ill or stress and anxiety had stolen my appetite.

Tonight, it was the latter.

We'd only been home from the set for a few hours, but I still couldn't shake the fact that some lunatic had found their way into my dressing room.

Me.

I had no idea who Me was. I didn't even have a list of possibilities.

All I knew was that this person was too close.

Between the flowers, the windshield incident, and now, a creepy candid picture inside my dressing room, I was officially freaked out.

I'd thought Levi had acted crazy talking about evidence and crime scenes when we were in the hospital parking lot, but this had put everything into perspective.

Worst-case scenarios? Yeah. I'd imagined at least one thousand of them. And that was just during the four or so mile drive home from the set.

Levi tapped my thigh with his hand. "You need to eat something."

I looked up at him and swam in the comfort of his blue eyes. "I'm not hungry," I whispered. "My stomach is in knots, and I'm having a bit of an internal freak-out at the moment."

He held me tighter. "What are you freaking out about?"

"*Me*," I whispered, and his lips pushed into a firm line at the mere sound of that normally innocuous two-letter word.

"You have nothing to worry about, okay?" he said, his voice reassuring and his big presence providing just enough solace that I could let my shoulders relax and release the tension pinching at my neck. "We've filed the police report. Every officer in a fifty-mile radius is aware, and you now have a security detail outside your door." He kissed my forehead softly, letting his lips linger for a long moment. "I won't let anything happen to you, okay?"

"But what about you?" I asked on a whisper, all of my worst fears coming to fruition. Sure, my anxiety was partially related to my well-being, but mostly, it revolved around the people I loved most in the world. Camilla and Levi were at the very top of that list.

"Don't you worry your pretty little head about me," he said, and a soft smile crested his lips. "I'm big and ugly enough to handle shit."

That made me giggle. "Big enough? Sure, I can definitely agree with that," I said and sat up straight to place a kiss to his lips. "But ugly enough? Hell to the no, you big, fat liar. Have you seen your eyes? Lord Almighty, they are a million miles away from being remotely close to ugly."

He grinned and tapped an index finger to the tip of my nose. "Ditto, baby. I'm a big fan of your eyes too."

"Hey, Ivy! Your phone is vibrating!" Camilla called from the kitchen, and a few seconds later, walked into the living room to toss me my cell.

I looked down at the screen to see several text message notifications.

Once I opened my inbox, I was face-to-face with a message from Boyce.

Boyce: Are you at your rental?

Me: Not sure why that matters, but yes. Why?

Boyce: Good. Get some sleep tonight. Last-minute reshoots tomorrow morning. Be on set by 9.

Me: What? Why? Hugo said we wrapped today.

Boyce: After I had a long discussion with Hugo, he has agreed to let me run the show for a few reshoots for the scene at Gaskins's house.

My jaw fell into my lap of its own accord. Was he being fucking serious right now?

Me: But Hugo was happy with everyone's performance...

Boyce: Like I said before, Hugo has given me the green light for reshoots tomorrow. Be there at 9. And make sure you get in bed early. I'd like to get these done within a few takes.

I felt like curling up into the fetal position and crying and screaming and breaking shit all at the same time. I stood up from the couch with a groan and kicked the afghan off my legs as I did.

"What's wrong?" Levi asked, and I started to pace the living room like a caged animal.

"Boyce just sent me messages about fucking reshoots. He says I need to be on set at nine a.m. tomorrow. What the fuck?" I questioned, and anger rose in my voice. "I feel like he's got it out for me!" I yelled, storming from the living room to my bedroom and dropping the weight of my body onto the bed.

My skin felt painful, anxiety prickling under the surface of it. I'd bled out everything I had to give emotionally for the scene at the house with Walter Gaskins. I'd given my heart and my soul, and I'd died for a cause I felt worthy.

But a reshoot felt like torture. As if, without the possibility to give more, I'd only be giving less. Not to mention, the things that Levi had told me and the way they changed how living out Grace's last breaths would feel.

I would sense the heartbeat of her baby within; I would be drawn to protect the womb.

"He doesn't have it out for you," Cam murmured after following me into the room and sitting on a hip beside me. She lifted a hand and stroked my back.

"He does, Cam," I insisted.

Her eyes were soft but stoic, and I knew without having to ask that she thought I was being dramatic about not wanting to do the scenes. Desperate, I shifted my focus from her to Levi, where he stood leaning against the doorframe to my room. His jaw was hard and lean body tense, even as he stood in supposed repose.

"He's got it out for her," he agreed, knowing I needed him to be on my side. "He's been riding her since day one, and I don't think it's based solely on performance."

"This is how producers are," Camilla argued.

"I can't do it," I whispered, the prospect of living it again slowing the beat of my heart. It felt needlessly torturous and superfluous. Hugo had been happy with the scene; he'd told me so himself.

But Boyce was like a dog with a bone, and he wouldn't give up on the idea of shooting it again.

"You don't have to."

Camilla shook her head, disagreeing completely. "Yes, she does. I know you guys are in that stage of your relationship where people shit rainbows and everything they say is right, but this is her job. And if they say she has to do a reshoot, she *has* to."

I looked at Cam, and she looked at me. I wanted her to take back her words, to agree with Levi and say I didn't have to do those stupid fucking reshoots.

But, she didn't.

"It'll be okay, Ivy. It's just one more day to push through," she added, before offering a sympathetic smile and heading out of my bedroom.

Just one more day to push through.

I hated that I agreed with her.

"God," I cried and sank my head into my hands. "She's right."

And she was. It didn't matter that I was personally attached to the story or the real-life people behind the characters now. It didn't matter that I'd given all I had to give for the scene and couldn't imagine I'd ever be able to do more.

I was the actress. I'd signed a contract and sold my opinions for a paycheck. It was my job to deliver, and I had to do it to their standards. If Boyce was demanding reshoots, I had to do them.

I didn't see Levi move, but I felt the warmth of his arms as they came around me reassuringly. "Ivy," he whispered right in the shell of my ear.

I wrapped my arms around the width of his back and squeezed in return, soaking in all of the comfort he had to give. It was ironic, really, seeking comfort from the man who'd actually been through the imaginary hell I was tired of living.

"I just need to sleep," I said, both to convince myself and him. Maybe if I could forget the day, put all of the chaos of pushy producers and possible stalkers to bed, I could wake up back in the perfect bliss of that morning.

Levi's lips on mine; the promise of the future bold and palpable.

"That's a good idea," Levi agreed.

He shifted away from our hug just enough and tucked the blankets around me. "I just have to run home and get some clothes, okay?"

A cold chill ran up my spine at the threat of his absence, but I shoved it aside and nodded.

He'd dropped everything to make sure I was protected and seen to, and he'd listened thoughtfully as I complained about my stupid, fantastical problems. Problems he'd actually *lived*.

"Okay," I agreed, steeling my voice to sound sure. I could give this to him. I could find the strength to be okay for the both of us.

Cam walked back in after a soft knock on the door, her hand a fist that she held out in front of her. "I thought some Tylenol PM might help you sleep."

I smiled my thanks and took them, tossing them back with ease and then reaching for the glass of water in her other hand. The cool liquid coated the column of my throat and soothed the burn of unknowns.

Cam took the glass back with a smile and stepped outside, and I settled back into the bed.

"I'll make sure Dane is good to go outside before I leave," Levi assured, rubbing a thumb over the smooth skin of my arm.

Fear curled my body into itself. I'd been ignoring the threat for so long, the potency had built in the meantime.

Officer Fox, ever the protector, didn't let it linger.

Levi's lips felt perfect and reassuring as they sealed to my own and opened and closed. My tongue peeked in the opening, just enough to touch the tip of his, and the air in my lungs suddenly felt fresher.

Like the weight of the day and the world would be lighter now that Levi was there to help me hold it.

I closed my eyes as he skirted a hand over my hip and stood up from the bed, and I did my best to calm my mind.

I pushed myself to think thoughts of beach days with an Adonis and little raven-haired babies. I wasn't ready for it now—the commitment, the marriage, the kids—but I loved the idea of someday.

Sleep ebbed and flowed like the roll of the tide, and when the last wave crashed, it was finally enough for the restorative water to pull me under.

To dream lives and dream men. Far away from the recurring nightmare.

CHAPTER
TWENTY-SEVEN

Levi

THE SOFT CLICK OF IVY'S DOOR SHUTTING BEHIND ME MADE CAM'S head come up from her spot on the couch. The hall was dark and long, and she waited for me to close the distance before breaking the silence.

"She asleep?" she asked.

I nodded. "Will be soon anyway."

"She's not normally this hysterical, honestly. It's kind of surprising to see her acting like—"

I shook my head and held up a hand, and Camilla stopped talking.

"I told her some things. About me. About Grace. I didn't really think about what that would do to her ability to act it out."

"What kinds of things?" she asked immediately, not nearly as careful with my feelings as her sister. For as weird as things had started between us, it was amazing how easily we'd fallen into sibling type roles.

I chuckled. "None of your business."

"Yeah, sure. She'll tell me if I ask her. She tells me everything."

I glanced over my shoulder, back down the hall, and pictured the woman who was so emotionally invested in my life—in the things I'd told her—that she was having anxiety attacks over putting herself back in the role of Grace.

My smirk was small but effective. "Not this, she won't."

Cam rolled her eyes and then moved them back to her book before asking, "I'm assuming you're staying the night?"

The floor creaked as I started moving again, a slow advance to the hook by the door where my coat hung.

"Yeah. After I run home real quick for a change of clothes."

"What's the matter? Not to the sleeping naked portion of the relationship yet?" she teased.

I shook my head and smiled as I pulled the door open. "I said a spare set of clothes. *Not* pajamas."

She stuck out her tongue and smiled, but I didn't wait for her to say anything else. Instead, I stepped outside and closed the door behind me.

"Hey, man," Dane greeted. "You headin' out?"

"I just have to run home, but I'll be back."

I noticed him nod in my periphery as I looked at the shining light through the mostly closed blinds. I thought about the women inside and fought against the pull in my gut. The flowers and the heart on the windshield and the gift in Ivy's dressing room. All of it felt like a record on repeat.

Flashes of the past taunted me with my mistakes and dared me to give love a go again. A vision of Grace on the floor of Walter Gaskins's kitchen made me close my eyes.

"You don't get distracted for a second, okay?" I ordered.

The bounce of Dane's head was enthusiastic as he assured me of his vigilance. "No worries, man. I got this."

With a clasp of his shoulder and a jerky nod, I moved away from the front door and climbed into my truck.

It started up quickly, and before I knew it, the cold air and the hot exhaust had mixed to close me in a white cloud of smoke. Eager to get home and back, I rushed the warm-up process and shifted into reverse.

The driveway was long, and I paused at the end to survey the surroundings. No lights, no sounds, the road was as abandoned as was to be expected on a weeknight at almost midnight.

Only the critters were active, glowing eyes and peeking positions at the side of the road as they ventured out for nighttime meals.

When the quiet became too much, I switched on the radio and pulled out of the drive, headed for home.

It was a short trip, about a mile and a half one way, but as the darkness yawned before me and as the distance between Ivy and me got larger, it felt like forever.

Unease and dread coated the end of "Blowing in the Wind" by Peter, Paul, and Mary, and I welcomed the change of song as it came to a close.

But the reprieve was short-lived.

The first notes of "Blue Bayou" were just as eerie as always, and my heart kicked into overdrive.

Goddamn, someone needs to outlaw this fucking song.

A flash caught my eye in the reflection in my mirror, and I slammed on the brakes to scout what I'd seen. Roy sang on about seeing his baby again, and my chest got tight.

With one swift move after another, I shifted into reverse and slammed my foot to the floor. The truck swung around violently, and I threw it into drive, back in the direction I'd come.

I couldn't describe my mania as anything more than a feeling, but feelings were *meant* to be felt.

Life and love and goddamn intuition didn't work as well when you were numb. Ivy had been the one to teach me that.

The driveway came up fast, and I took the turn entirely too quickly.

Gravel sprayed as I sped up the long road to the end and slid to a stop right behind Dane's cruiser.

The front of the house was noticeably empty, and my eyes scoured the siding desperately for the contrast of Dane's dark uniform.

I didn't even bother with closing the door as I climbed from the truck and rushed back up onto the front porch and straight for the front door.

I had my hand to the knob, ready to enter, when a glint of light pierced me in the eye from the bush at the side of the porch. I moved slowly, cautiously, to the edge and put to my hand to my gun at the side of my hip.

Brown leaves and leftover snow, the landscaping was a perfect depiction of the cold mess our little town fell into every winter.

But there was something else there, among the shrubbery and ice.

Blond hair and innocent, open eyes—and a five-inch slash across his throat.

Fuck. Oh God, *no*.

With no time to mourn Dane now, I swore to do it later as I moved back to the front door and pushed my way into the house.

The crack of the door against the wall startled the man and woman wrestling on the couch into a spin, and the knife in his hand settled on her creamy white throat.

"Levi!" she yelled, startled eyes and determination coloring her face bright pink.

I lifted my gun and trained it on the intruder.

"What the fuck is going on here?" I asked, trying to calm the surge of adrenaline enough to figure out the answer. "Boyce?"

His eyes were wild and his appearance disheveled as he pushed the large, already bloodied blade farther into her delicate throat.

"She's mine," he said softly, all traces of sane Hollywood producer gone. He'd been replaced by a desperate psychopath. "I've seen you with her, but I'm the one she's meant to be with."

Red hair and green eyes and with all the threat to life I could handle, I closed one eye and lined up the shot, right in the middle of Boyce's eyes. As soon as I was sure I could hit him clean, I'd take it.

"Please, Boyce," she said. "Camilla's sleeping."

My heart seized.

"Can't we go somewhere and talk about this?"

His laugh was manic. "Now? *Now,* you want to talk?"

I pulled back on the trigger slightly, ready with just a tap as soon as he gave me the opportunity.

They were too fucking close together, her head just slightly in front of his, and desperation ran hot inside my veins as I strived to find an open shot.

But Boyce knew my challenge and did everything in his power to keep them in motion while holding the knife firmly beside her neck.

They bobbed and they weaved, and then…it was too late.

Too late to talk.

"It's too late to talk. You should have thought about that before. The only way you're leaving here, leaving me, is *dead.*"

Too late to stop him.

Boyce's arm moved swiftly and without warning, dragging across her throat just as I pulled the trigger. Both of them hit the floor together.

Nothing but agony and prayer, I ran for the two of them and fell to my knees in a pool of blood. It was large, warm, and growing, and my hands shook as it coated them.

"Oh God, no," I cried, hoarse and depleted, slippery hands covering the wound and feeling for a pulse.

Slow already and slowing by the second, the beat faded under my fingers like a passing gust of wind.

Nothing would ever be the same, and everything I loved was

right back where it'd started.

Destroyed. Broken. Gone forever.

All I'd wanted was a second chance.

What I got was a repeat.

This isn't the end.
Coming Soon
May 20th, 2018
FOX
The Final Installment of the Stone Cold Fox Trilogy.

PREORDER FOX TODAY
**If you continue reading, there is an exclusive excerpt from FOX
waiting for you at the end! ☺**

Also, if you feel like you need some fellow reader support to get
you through until Fox releases, there is an exclusive spoiler group to
discuss all things Levi and Ivy and this angsty AF trilogy!
Feel free to curse our names and scream out your frustrations. Lol.
Join here: www.facebook.com/groups/347384075758996

2018 has been the start of ALL THE FUN THINGS.
Find out why everyone is laughing their ass off every Monday
morning with us and stay up to date with all of our news by signing
up for our newsletter:
www.authormaxmonroe.com/newsletter

You may live to regret much, but we promise it won't be this.
If you're already signed up, consider sending us a message to tell us
how much you love us. We really like that. ;)

Follow us online:
Website: www.authormaxmonroe.com
Facebook: www.facebook.com/authormaxmonroe
Reader Group: www.facebook.com/groups/1561640154166388
Twitter: www.twitter.com/authormaxmonroe
Instagram: www.instagram.com/authormaxmonroe
Goodreads: goo.gl/8VUIz2

ACKNOWLEDGMENTS

First of all, THANK YOU for reading. That goes for anyone who's bought a copy, read an ARC, helped us beta, edited, formatted, or found time in their busy schedule to help us out in any way.

We love you guys. Every single one of you. Your love, your support, your enthusiasm for our words is *everything*.

So, THANK YOU.

Thank for you reading.

Thank you for supporting us.

Thank you. Thank you. Thank you.

THANK YOU.

(Sorry. Monroe gets repetitive when she REALLY means something.)

Without every single one of you, none of this would be possible.

We know this series is different from our romantic comedies.

We also know Levi and Ivy's story has put you through the proverbial ringer at times.

But, just trust us, you will get everything you want and all the things you didn't even know you wanted in the final book of the Stone Cold Fox Trilogy.

Fox is coming for you very soon! May 20th, to be exact!

And, we realized the ending of COLD has probably left you like WHAT THE FLUFFING FLUFF??

So, we've added a little sneak peek of FOX below.

All our love,
Max & Monroe

COMING SOON: MAY 20TH, 2018

FOX

BOOK THREE IN THE STONE COLD FOX TRILOGY

Some things are meant to be; some *aren't*.

I never thought this would be my life.
I never believed I could feel this way.

I don't know where to go from here.
I never want to be anywhere else.

My whole world has changed.
She is my whole world.

I'm not sure how to be me again.
I've never felt more like myself.

I've never needed anyone, but I need him.
I love her. I'll always love her.

But is our love enough? Can Levi and I really survive this?
Together, Ivy and I can survive anything.

FOX EXCERPT

Levi

MY HEART THRUMMED PAINFULLY AS I PULLED IVY CLOSER TO MY chest and put my lips to her hair.

She was silent, and the expression on her face couldn't be described as anything other than lost. Jagged red lines broke the smooth white surface of her eyes, and an angry blush swallowed up the normally perfect skin of her cheeks. Her body was in the throes of a meltdown.

But that wasn't a surprise. Half of her soul—Camilla's half—had been severed and battered, and was, right then, struggling to hold on through a set of trauma doors and unyielding concrete walls.

As identical twins, Camilla and Ivy were bound together by ties that were supernatural and inexplicably complicated.

They'd been born of the same egg, housed in the same mother, and lived a cherished life together. But now, they'd been forced to fend for themselves. Camilla fought for her life, and Ivy was left to stand by and do nothing.

I knew the torture of helplessness. I'd known it with Grace, and now, I knew it all over again as I watched Ivy lock herself inside and completely shut down emotionally because she'd couldn't aid in the physical fight for her sister.

"Levi," the chief greeted, his voice softened by grief. He gave me an affectionate squeeze of the shoulder with one hand and continued to hold his wife closer with the other.

They'd just arrived, the first of the crowd of support I knew would gather at Ivy's and my sides. Margo had been sobbing on the way over here—I could tell by the mottle of her face and throat and the moisture in her eyes—but she'd pulled it together before entering the building for the sake of Ivy and for the sake of the town.

We were well-versed in disaster. Our strength, it seemed, was in our ability to stand beside one another despite it.

I noticed the dried blood that coated my hands as I smoothed them down the rigid lines of Ivy's arms and pulled her even closer.

She was in shock, had been since the moment I'd abruptly woken her from a sleep aid-enhanced slumber and told her the news that had brought us here.

Cool blood still lay on the floor of the house we'd left, and police still swarmed over the bodies of Boyce Williams and Dane Marx, collecting evidence.

But the blood could wait. It would wait until we had word on Camilla, and Ivy had anything and everything she needed.

From this moment on, I was a man at her disposal. I'd be her punching bag when she needed and her shoulder to cry on when she allowed. For her, I vowed to be anything and everything. *Always.*

Moments after it had all gone down, mere seconds after I'd fired a bullet straight between Boyce Williams's eyes, I'd been unwilling and unable to admit to Camilla's end. Not there, next to the man she'd been willing to face head on in an effort to protect her sister. Not in the house where she'd spent those moments in terror, waiting for me to save her.

Not while her sister slept unwittingly in the next room.

And now, all I could was pray.

Pray for Camilla. Pray for Ivy. Pray for a fucking miracle.

The door to the trauma unit opened swiftly, and a doctor came through, still pulling her mask from her face. Her surgical scrubs were covered in blood, and the look on her face would be burned in my mind for the rest of eternity.

"Camilla Stone's family?" she asked, bone-weary and broken.

I knew the words before she spoke them. I'd lived them before. But Ivy, *sweet fucking Ivy*, still had a relationship with hope.

She hadn't seen Camilla before the ambulance took her.

"Yes." Ivy's voice was scratchy and dry from the screams and wails and subsequent nonuse. Her agony had been physical as I'd told her the news. Potent. Piercing. "That's me. I'm her sister," she said. "And our parents are in LA, but they're trying to catch a red-eye flight out here."

My throat thick with saliva, I did my best to steady myself, hooking my arms around Ivy's body.

I knew when the words came—words that would change everything she'd ever known—she'd need the support.

Direct and professional, the doctor stepped forward to Ivy and made eye contact, but she worried the mask in her hand with her fingers. "I'm Dr. Ines," she introduced herself, and Ivy nodded and swallowed, unable to say anything else.

"Your sister came in with a severe laceration to her throat and had lost a significant amount of blood volume. We rushed her to the operating room, started a transfusion, but we lost her on the table. We defibrillated for twenty minutes, but I'm...I'm sorry. She didn't make it."

High-pitched and soul-destroying, the wail Ivy let out was the likes of which I would never recover from. It keened and moaned, and utter devastation rattled at its core.

She was a half of a whole now, and she'd never find the missing piece.

"Oh, Ivy," I murmured, pulling her close and spilling into the abyss of guilt.

The bottomless pit of blackness that taunted I could have done something more—that I could have stopped it if I'd taken it all more seriously from the beginning.

Hell, I hadn't even told Ivy the heroic decision Camilla had made to protect her.

But it wasn't out of secrecy; it was because I knew, in this moment, Ivy wouldn't be able to handle the truth of her sister's sacrifice.

God, I'd give anything to change this, to remedy the pain Ivy would never release, but I was powerless.

Helpless to alter the past and unable to protect the future.

All I could do was live this *with* her, be present *for* her, and pray for God's grace.

We couldn't take any more hits.

We couldn't take any more surprises.

Though, as the ones left behind—no matter what came—we had no choice but to survive.

And I'd spend the rest of my life making sure we did it *together.*

Made in the USA
Middletown, DE
18 July 2021

44365998R00116